J ust then, I heard a voice. I'm not sure where it came from. Maybe the sky, or from somewhere inside me. I couldn't tell. "I will help you," it said. The voice was sweet and comforting, like my Grandma Zoe's.

"Who are you?" I asked softly, just in case I might get an answer.

The clouds shifted back into an angel shape. I shook my head in disbelief.

"There's your angel again, Hannah," Ian called.

I gasped. Ian had seen it, too!

I had an angel! I actually had an angel who sent me messages by clouds and stars! She had a voice like Grandma Zoe's. And right then and there, I knew her name...

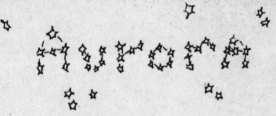

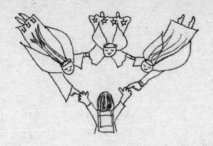

Hannah and the Angels

Mission Down Under

by Linda Lowery Keep

Based on a concept by
Linda Lowery Keep
and Carole Newhouse

Random House 🏠 New York

Copyright © 1998 by Renegade Angel, Inc., and
Newhouse/Haft Associates, Inc.
HANNAH AND THE ANGELS is a trademark of Random House, Inc.,
Renegade Angel, Inc., and Newhouse/Haft Associates, Inc.
All rights reserved under International and Pan-American Copyright
Conventions. Published in the United States by Random House, Inc.,
New York, and simultaneously in Canada by Random House of
Canada Limited, Toronto.

http://www.randomhouse.com/

Library of Congress Cataloging-in-Publication Data
Keep, Linda Lowery.
Hannah and the angels: mission down under / by Linda Lowery Keep
SUMMARY: During a chaotic music class in school, Hannah finds
herself mysteriously transported to Australia, sent there by the angels
that watch over her to help her new friend, Ian, track down poachers
that are preying on endangered animals.
ISBN 0-679-89081-5
[1. Angels—Fiction. 2. Space and time—Fiction. 3. Adventures and
adventurers—Fiction. 4. Poaching—Fiction. 5. Australia—Fiction.] I. Title.
II. Series: Keep, Linda Lowery. Hannah and the angels: bk #1
PZ7.K25115Mi 1998 [Fic]—dc21 97-39285

Printed in the United States of America
10 9 8 7 6 5 4 3 2

I dedicate this series to my angels,
who guided me all the way.

Acknowledgments

I am forever grateful to the many people who believed in this vision and supported me beyond imagining, especially:

Lisa Banim, my extraordinary editor, whose endless faith, professional expertise, and dedicated hours gave this project wings;

Kathy Garcia, whose generosity, humor, and amazing vitality eased me through the long birthing process of these books;

My research trackers, including Craig Hoover, who battles illegal poaching through the World Wildlife Fund's Traffic USA division; the folks at the Aussie Help Line in Los Angeles, who had all the answers; Sarah Fassett, a Tasmanian exchange student at Boulder High School who kept my Aussie talk authentic; all the aboriginal artists and musicians who inspired me;

Carole Newhouse, who introduced this project to Random House and who has led me to new insights in my life;

My real-world angels, who have been so generous and constant every mile of the way: Mick Lowery, Ruth Skafsgaard, Dave and Pam Lowery, Judith Fisher, Rob and Mary Cleminson, Emily Kelley, Leiah Boutelle, Cid Lowery, Ed Douglas, Randy Fowler, Don and Leslie Kaniecki, and my true-blue buddy Eileen Lucas, whose support never faltered from the moment the angels planted the seeds of these books in my heart so many years ago.

Contents

Hannah and the Angels

Mission Down Under

Chapter 1

Dreamtime, Ms. Crybaby, and an Upside-Down Flute

I was born to fly. My Grandma Zoe knew it right away. She says that when I was little, I'd flap my arms in my crib like a baby bird wanting to take off.

I believe her. In fact, I have a theory that maybe I was flying like the aboriginal people in Australia do. They stand perfectly still, with their feet planted on the ground, while their spirits fly. They call it traveling in the dreamtime. *I* call it flying in my crib.

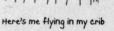

cute hair

Here's me flying in my crib

Katie, my best friend, thinks stuff like that is just amazing. Her twin brother, David (my second-best friend), doesn't.

"You're so gullible," he said once. He loves to use words he thinks I don't understand. "Those stories are nothing but fairy tales."

(Here's how I picture those people flying in the dreamtime)

"Just because there are some things you can't see on your stupid computer screen doesn't mean they don't exist," Katie told him.

That's when David put on his earphones and started drumming his fingers to the music like Katie and I didn't exist anymore. Not that David's always a jerk. Here are some good things about David:

1. He's a really good chess player and never cheats.
2. If anything drastic happens to Katie, David stays right by her side. (Like when she fractured her tibia jazz-dancing and had to go to the emergency room.)
3. He has the best eyelashes in the entire sixth grade.

DAVID'S EYELASHES

Front View   Top View

(I've never actually seen this view of David, so it's tricky to draw)

Anyway, I'd better get on with this story. As you can probably tell already, I never think in a straight line. David says my brain waves jump across the tops of thought groups, like nerve messages jumping across synapses. I like it when he says things like that. In case you didn't notice, he's also very smart. That's one more good thing about him.

This whole thing with the angels began one day in music class. It was truly the most amazing and unexpected thing that has ever happened to me. Much more amazing than flying in my crib.

Here's how I started out that day

It was a regular Tuesday afternoon and we were playing some stupid marching song written by some dull old guy to celebrate war.

Then Jimmy Fudge, who plays bassoon next to me, starts running his fingernail on the blackboard behind him, making an awful scraping noise. He does this annoying thing where he plays a note, scritches a note, plays a note, scritches a note…You get the picture. So none of us can play our instruments because we're all shuddering from the scritching, and the whole class starts playing flat.

Jimmy Fudge

"He's scritching again, Ms. C.!" Carl Jones yells.

The boys have a contest going to see who can make Ms. Crysler lose it first. She's such an easy target, it's just plain sad.

Then someone else hollers, "Hey, Fudge! Did you grow your fingernail extra long just to do that?"

"Sure did," Jimmy yells back, showing off his nails. They do look pretty long. They're really dirty, too.

Then Kevin McPherson picks up the eraser from the blackboard and gives Fudge skunk hair. You know: a white chalk streak down the middle of his head. That's the prize awarded to the winner of the "Dude of the Day" contest. (Jimmy Fudge wins a lot.)

That was the last straw for Ms. Crysler. (We call her Ms. Crybaby.)

She's doomed to teach 6th grade forever

"Stop it! Stop it!" she cries. She pulls out her hanky and blows her nose really hard. "I've never had such a rude and disruptive class in all my years of teaching!"

Ms. Crybaby

I feel kind of sorry for Ms. Crybaby. She just can't handle the pressure of sixth graders, so she cries a lot—which, as you can imagine, all the boys love. She needs to go back to teaching second grade, which is what she begs the superintendent for at the end of every school year. But no one else wants to teach sixth grade, I guess.

So I decide to take advantage of the situation. I like to play my flute upside down, which I think is an amazing and wonderful trick. Ms. Crybaby thinks it's a problem I'll outgrow. She's a rules person. I'm not. If I want to play a half note longer than I should, I do. So what? That's how I express myself. It drives Ms. Crybaby crazy.

I turn my flute upside down and start playing

this Mozart piece I really like. But just when I hit the E, which is my favorite note, something really bizarre happens. A different kind of music starts coming out, not at all like the E on my flute. It's a mysterious, far-off kind of sound, like it came floating from an ancient time.

E is my favorite note on the flute

I quickly take the flute from my lips and look around. Everything is complete chaos. Ms. Crybaby is totally out of control, and Jimmy Fudge is making a power fist like an Olympic champion, all proud of his skunk hair. Nobody even notices me.

I try another upside-down E. Sure enough, sounds come out like moon music, or maybe a lullaby I heard before I was even born. They whirl around me, making me dizzy.

And then it happened. The most amazing and unexpected thing that I was telling you about. Right then, on a Tuesday afternoon, in the middle of the "Screeching Crybaby March" at Kennedy Middle School...

Chapter 2

※※※ ※※※ ※※※

Didgeridoo and Who Are You?

Suddenly, there was dead silence. No more Jimmy Fudge, no more Ms. Crybaby.

My flute was really heavy. I went to set it down, and I noticed the most peculiar thing. It wasn't a flute anymore! It was a gigantic wooden tube, with little pictures all over it—the kind you see in caves, all scratchy and primitive-looking.

I looked around. It was night, and the sky was packed with stars. I mean *really* packed—there were more stars than I even knew existed. Wait a minute...Something awful must have happened to me! Like maybe Jimmy Fudge had smacked me in the head with his bassoon and I'd been knocked unconscious. I mean, I *was* seeing stars, right?

DIDGERIDOO
(Of course, the artists don't put the designs on until the ants are finished eating!)

I could still hear that ancient music playing faintly, as if it were traveling across centuries. Right now I was standing in a cluster of trees. I peeked through the tall white trunks and saw two people in the distance, sitting by a fire. There was an old man with bushy white hair, playing one of those peculiar tubes like the one I was holding. Across from him was a boy, probably thirteen or fourteen, wearing a cowboy hat.

I leaned against a tree and closed my eyes to calm myself down. I must have sucked in too much oxygen in music class, playing my flute upside down. Was I hyperventilating? As soon as I pulled myself together, I was sure I'd be back in the middle of the "Dude of the Day" craziness.

But when I opened my eyes, they were still there—the boy, the man, the fire, the stars.

Me

I thought I'd try to see if I could walk. My feet seemed to work okay, so I headed toward the fire.

"Who are you?" I asked the boy. For some reason, I didn't feel that scared. After all, it was *my* dream.

"I'm Ian," he said. "And that's George," he added, nodding toward the old man.

I probably looked all frazzled and confused, as if I'd just escaped from the local zoo. But these guys didn't seem the least bit surprised that I'd walked up to them out of nowhere.

"I'm Hannah," I said.

The boy didn't answer right away. He looked at me for a moment or two, as if he was sizing me up. "So you play the didgeridoo, Hannah?" he asked.

It sounded like he was reading from Dr. Seuss: *When you went to Timbuktu, did you meet a Did-Jury-Doo?*

"The *what?*" I said.

"Your instrument," said Ian, pointing. "The one in your hand."

"Oh!" I said, feeling stupid. "No. I play the flute."

"Well, then, mate," he said with a grin, "sit down and have a go at it!"

I must admit, Ian had a very cute way of talking. If this was a dream, I figured I could go along with it. I sat down on the ground—which was hard as a rock, by the way—and copied the way George was holding his instrument.

"This thing looks like an old tree limb," I said.

"It is," said Ian. "It's made from a eucalyptus tree. The ants eat out the insides until it's hollow."

"Ants?" I repeated quickly, pushing the instrument far away from my mouth.

"White ants," Ian explained. "Termites."

I peered down the tube to see if the little buggers were squirming around down there. I had no intention of swallowing a mouthful of termites, even in a dream.

"Go ahead, try it," Ian coaxed. "No worries, mate. The ants moved out long ago."

I blew into the didgeridoo, but all that came out was air.

"Try buzzing your lips," Ian said. "Like this: *Pfffttt.*"

I *pfffttt*ed. Nothing happened. "I can't do it!" I hollered down the tube in frustration. "It doesn't work!"

My voice echoed. It sounded very mysterious, so I yelled again. "Get me out of this dream! Send me back!"

Just then, I heard a voice answer—and it wasn't mine. It swished around in the didgeridoo like wind.

"When...you...finish-sh-sh-sh," it whispered.

I know what you're thinking. You think I have a screw loose, that I've got bats in my brains. Well, I don't blame you. This is very weird stuff I'm telling you about. But I really did hear a voice.

I called back down the tube, "Finish *what?*"

I heard a *whoosh-whoosh* blow through the didgeridoo, like leaves in the wind. I pressed my ear against the opening as if I were listening to a seashell. The voice spoke again, all soft and hushed: "Your...misssssssion."

Can you tell I couldn't believe what I was hearing?

YOUR MISSSSSION

I froze. What was going on? My eyes darted to Ian and then to George. They acted as if they hadn't heard anything. I touched my knees and my face and the ground. This was really me, Hannah Martin. And I was really here—wherever *that* was.

"Where am I, Ian?" I asked.

"That's easy, mate," he said smiling. "The Australian Outback."

"Outback?" I frowned. This wasn't making sense.

"Right. You're in the Land Down Under. In the desert. The bush."

"That's impossible!" I cried, dropping the didgeridoo and leaping to my feet.

How could I be in music class one minute, and halfway around the world the next? I started running around like a wild animal, touching trees, touching rocks. I couldn't be in Australia! Unless, of course... *No!* It couldn't be! Had something really awful happened in music class? Like the most horrible, terrible, unpredictable thing of all? Could I have had a...heart attack?

"Impossible," I whimpered. I wasn't even twelve yet!

Could I actually be...*dead?*

Impossible!!!

Chapter 3

Flies for Breakfast

"Nothing is impossible," came a deep voice.

For a second, I thought it was God. All the mean, awful things I'd ever done in my life flashed through my mind. Then I calmed down and realized it was George who was talking to me.

"*This* is impossible," I repeated, crossing my arms stubbornly.

George sat very still. His skin was all shiny brown in the firelight, and his beard glowed white. "If you want answers to your questions, you must be silent," he said, his black eyes gleaming.

George

That made no sense. None of this whole dream, or whatever it was, did. I felt like Alice in Wonderland.

"You don't understand," I said. "I need to—"

The old man cut me off. "Silence is the only way to learn the answers to your questions."

He had the kind of voice that's quiet but full of authority. When teachers use that voice, even the worst kids sit down and behave.

So I shut up. As you can imagine, that's not an easy thing for me. Ian, who wasn't paying any attention at all to me now, stoked the fire. George went back to his didgeridoo.

I began to feel fidgety. I didn't hear any more *whooshes* or voices, so I decided to write all of this down in my journal. It's kind of like a diary, but it has pictures, too. I keep track of everything important that happens to me, day and night. I'm very organized and serious about it. Katie says it's because I have a Virgo moon. I have different sections for stuff like "Dreams" and "Actions and Consequences" and "What I Want." Right now, two of the "What I Want" listings are:

—Fuzzy socks to match my lavender vest
—To sail across the Atlantic Ocean, solo (except I'd take Frank with me—he's my dog)

I zipped open my backpack to get my journal. Oops, wait! I completely forgot to tell you something important. My backpack was with me when I appeared in the trees. I knew it was mine, because it was red, and my special signature with the stars that I'd written in purple ink was right there on the inside flap.

Anyway, when I opened my backpack, I got another surprise. It was full of stuff I'd never seen before! I couldn't tell everything that was in it because of the dark, but here are some of the things I found:

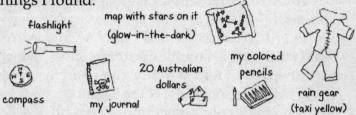

flashlight

map with stars on it
(glow-in-the-dark)

my colored
pencils

compass

20 Australian
dollars

my journal

rain gear
(taxi yellow)

Ian peered over my shoulder. "You got a swag in there?" he asked.

"What's a swag?" I said.

"It's a kind of sleeping bag we use out here in the bush."

I rummaged around in my pack. "I don't think I have one," I said. "My pack isn't *that* big."

"You can use mine," Ian said. "I can sleep on a blanket."

He walked over to a Jeep that was parked nearby and tossed me a bundle. He threw George another bundle, took out a blanket, and spread it out on the ground.

I unrolled the swag, which was a canvas mat with big flaps for a cover. When I got inside, I felt like a bug in a rug, with my head sticking out. I lay there quietly for a long time, staring at all the stars. It's weird that when it's the dead of night in Australia, it's afternoon back home.

"Ian," I said, pointing at the sky. "Does that constellation look like a snake to you?"

"To be sure," he agreed. "And a very large snake at that."

"And over there, that one looks like a lizard. You see it?" I asked.

He did. We also spotted a bird with a parrot beak. And later I saw the Southern Cross, which David once told me you can't see in North America, only below the equator.

the Southern Cross

Suddenly, something scary and lonely-sounding howled in the distance. I pulled the flaps of my swag tight.

"It's just a dingo, Hannah," Ian said. "A wild dog."

Whatever it was, it sounded huge. And hungry.

"It won't bother us," Ian added. "Dingoes don't really like people."

Just to be safe, I fumbled in my backpack for my heavy metal flashlight. Maybe I could fend off an attacking dingo with it if I needed to. I lay with my eyes wide open, worrying.

"So what's all this about a 'mission'?" I whispered into the darkness. I wasn't sure if I was talking to myself or to the stars.

Right then, a few stars seemed to sway and slowly shift around. As they changed places, I watched, totally amazed, as they spelled out: A-U-R-O-R-A. Then they moved back to their original places.

Magic Star Message: Aurora

I quickly scribbled the word in my notebook so I wouldn't forget. I also wrote down "didgeridoo, swag, dingo." I'm not sure why. It just seemed like the right thing to do. Like I told you, I write down *everything*.

Just then, the dingo howled again.

"Ian?" I called nervously. "George?"

They were both asleep. I lay perfectly still, clutching my flashlight. In the distance, I could hear more dingoes joining the first one, howling like lost wolves in the night. After a while, I started to get kind of used to them.

The next thing I knew, it was morning. Or at least it was in my dream. I woke up scratching— my face, my arms, my hair. And when I opened my eyes, I leaped straight out of my swag. Flies! My skin was crawling with flies! I started stomping my feet and running around in circles.

"Get these bugs *off* me!" I shouted.

We were in the middle of a major fly attack. Swarms of flies blackened the air, ready to dive-bomb. I'd never seen anything like it. George was by the fire, head to toe in flies. He didn't seem disturbed at all. How could he stand there, all calm like that?

I threw the swag over me. I must have looked like a Halloween ghost. At least I couldn't see all those gross flies anymore. But I could hear them buzzing.

"Aren't they bugging you?" I asked, peeking

out with one eye.

George shrugged. "No use fighting them," he said. He handed me a hunk of bread that he'd toasted over the fire. I grabbed it quickly so the flies couldn't get it, and hid it under the swag.

Ian came over beside me. "The aboriginal people believe all animals have a good purpose. Flies lick the dirt and grime off our bodies."

Yuck! My mouth dropped open. I shut it quickly so no flies could get in.

"It's rather like a bath," George said, smiling.

"A bath? I don't think so!" I mumbled through the canvas. "No bath for me today!"

FLY BATH
(not exactly relaxing)

Still swatting like a maniac, I made a beeline for the Jeep. I jumped inside and stayed there for a long time, hiding under my swag. Then I remembered the toast. I checked it for flies and shoved it in my mouth.

"What am I doing here?" I moaned to Ian when he came up. "I'm supposed to be in school today!" The bread was really dry. I was spitting crumbs all over the place.

"We'll talk about it on the way," Ian said. He threw my pack in the back of the Jeep.

"What do you mean, 'talk about it'?" I asked. "Talk about what?"

"Our adventure," he said. "The one you and I are going on."

"What adventure?" I said. "And where exactly are we going?"

"Let's just say we'll be escaping the flies, mate," he answered, winking.

George and Ian put out the fire and began to pack up.

A sudden thought hit me like a thunderbolt. *What was I doing, going off in a Jeep with two guys I didn't even know? Shouldn't I be scared?* I had to think fast. I slipped my notebook from my pack and flipped to: "Actions and Consequences."

I wrote furiously:

Action #1:	Stay here.
Consequences:	I'll be left in the middle of nowhere, will be lonely and hungry, and may get eaten by flies or dingoes.
Action #2:	Go with George and Ian.
Consequences:	I'll have an adventure, maybe end up kidnapped, possibly murdered in a brutal, unspeakable way, my body left to rot in the Australian desert. Then the flies and dingoes will get me anyway.
Action #3:	Get to a phone. Now.
Consequences:	I can get help from my parents or the police.

I put a checkmark beside choice #3. There was just one problem. There were no phones in the Outback. I'd have to go with these guys and hope we'd get to a town soon.

There was one other possibility. I could wake myself up from this weird dream.

I pinched myself. It didn't work.

Chapter 4

A Sign in the Sky

George started the Jeep, and we headed out across the rocky desert. Just like that. I mean, there was no road. The three of us were bouncing around inside the Jeep like Mexican jumping beans. I kept bumping my head on the roof. It hurt, too.

"Grab the bar in front of you!" Ian shouted from the back. I held on tight.

For such a quiet guy, George was one wild driver. We were speeding over all the bumps so fast that our backsides were a mile off the seats half the time.

"So, Hannah, what do you know about poachers?" Ian shouted to me.

"Poachers?" I shouted back. Ian was a lot like David. I was getting tired of all these new words I didn't know. Poachers sounded like some kind of eggs.

"Smugglers, mate!" he yelled. "People who steal endangered animals from the wild and sell them for money."

Well, *that* was pretty horrible. "Are you and George poachers?" I figured I might as well ask.

Ian laughed, and even George let out a whoop. "That'll be the day, huh, George?" Ian said. "No, Hannah, this bloke here has captured more poachers in the bush than anybody. Caught 'em red-handed stuffing crocodiles right into their bags."

"Wow!" I said, impressed. George was a surprising person, all right. What a dangerous way to make a living!

"So you prowl around the Outback, hunting down bad guys?"

"It's called tracking," Ian explained. "And George here is a tracker. He's heading off on a special mission."

"Mission?" I asked, raising my eyebrows. There was that word again.

"Yeah, he's on the trail of some particularly nasty python poachers. Nobody's been able to catch any of them yet."

"Pythons? As in snakes?" I asked George eagerly. Unlike many people, I happen to be a snake lover. I've always wanted to go to India someday and learn to charm a cobra.

"That's right, mate," George

answered. "Smugglers can get forty thousand dollars for a rare python. You have to be smart. Catch the nasty blokes at their own game, you know?"

"Sounds exciting," I said, nodding.

"Good," said Ian.

"What do you mean, 'good'?" I said.

"Oh, I just mean..." His voice trailed off. "You know, it's rather interesting that we saw animals in the stars last night," he said, changing the subject.

"It is?" I said.

"Pythons, lizards, parrots—they're all endangered here in Australia," Ian said.

I opened my mouth to say something and got a mouthful of gritty road dust. My tongue felt like I could sandpaper a wall with it.

"What's an aurora?" I asked.

Ian heard me wrong. "Anaconda?" he yelled.

"No." I know what *that* is—an enormous snake. I saw a movie about one once. "Never mind," I said with a sigh. I had a feeling the aurora thing had nothing to do with Ian. I didn't exactly want to drag him into my crazy visions of shifting stars and a talking didgeridoo.

"It's too noisy to hear much back here!" Ian shouted. "We can talk more when we stop somewhere."

It took us a long time to stop anywhere. Five hours to be exact, according to my watch, which was now mysteriously set to Australian time. It took that long because there was not one house or gas station the whole way. In the meantime, we tried a car game.

"I'm thinking of an animal that begins with a K," I began loudly.

Ian got *koala* right away. That was my first and last turn. George and Ian kept doing Australian animals I'd never heard of: *skink*, which they said was a lizard; *lorikeet*, which they said was a really colorful parakeet; and *wallaby*. That was the one animal I knew and would have gotten, but George beat me to it.

koala

skink

rainbow lorikeet

I hate playing games with people who use words I don't know. It really gets me furious if I don't have a chance to jump in. For a while, I stared out the open window and watched the landscape bump by. It was red and flat, like a different planet. The clouds were huge. One of them looked like an angel flying alongside the Jeep.

my angel cloud

kangaroo bar
(in case you hit a
kangaroo by accident,
the Jeep won't get totaled)

termite hills
(as tall as me)

I turned back to Ian and pointed at the cloud. "Look!" I shouted.

"It almost looks like an angel," he said. "Don't you think so?"

I nodded and stared at the cloud, mulling over my situation. Shifting stars. Mission. Ian. George. Endangered animals. Poachers. Weird voices and angel clouds. Could it be that they were all connected—and I was somehow a part of this whole thing, too? Was I on a kind of mission?

An angel cloud-wing began to drift just then, floating into three parts. I swear it turned into the letters "Y-E-S."

Yes, what? I thought. *Yes, I'm on an endangered animal mission?*

On the other hand, it could be I was going loony. Not only didn't I know a single thing about poaching or Australia, but I was also beginning to believe that clouds were answering my questions. How nuts was that?

George turned and smiled at me, as if he knew what I was thinking.

"Remember what I told you about asking questions in silence?" he said. "You look like you're beginning to get some answers." He chuckled.

Just then, I heard a voice. I'm not sure where it came from. Maybe the sky, or from somewhere inside me. I couldn't tell. "I will help you," it said. The voice was sweet and comforting, like my Grandma Zoe's.

"Who are you?" I asked softly, just in case I might get an answer.

The clouds shifted back into an angel shape. I shook my head in disbelief.

"There's your angel again, Hannah," Ian called.

I gasped. Ian had seen it, too!

I had an angel! I actually had an angel who sent me messages by clouds and stars! She had a voice like Grandma Zoe's. And right then and there, I knew her name.

Aurora.

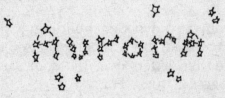

Chapter 5

A Coffin with Your Cheesecake?

We got out at a wooden building with a sign outside that read TINY'S TUCKERBAG. Another sign with faded red letters over the door said FOOD * PETROL * BEER * GUNS. For the middle of nowhere, this place was hopping. It was full of people chowing down, surrounded by camping gear, boomerangs (I'll tell you about those later), and souvenirs.

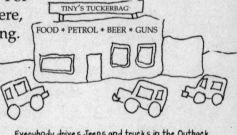

Everybody drives Jeeps and trucks in the Outback

George, Ian, and I found an empty booth with a red-checkered tablecloth. I scanned the place for a phone. There was one in the corner! That made me so happy. Then I saw the torn piece of paper

24

taped to it that said OUT OF ORDER. Now I was *not* happy.

"What'll it be, George?" the man behind the counter called out. He was enormous, the size of a gorilla, with a deep tan. I knew instantly he had to be Tiny. "I owe you one, mate," he added, his blue eyes twinkling. "The tucker's on me." I figured out pretty quickly that *tucker* means "food" in Australia. A tuckerbag is what you carry your food in when you're in the bush.

tuckerbag

George ordered steaks all around. Until right then, I'd never understood how anyone could down an entire steak in one sitting. When they came, they were humongous, hanging off the edges of our platters. I had no problem scarfing mine down, though. I was starving.

George carried his plate over to the counter so he could chat with Tiny. It looked as if they were talking business. I couldn't help wondering what big thing Tiny owed George for. Or maybe three huge steaks weren't that expensive in Australia.

"So where are we going?" I asked Ian casually. But in the back of my mind I was thinking about where I might find the next phone.

Ian glanced around to make sure no one would hear us. "Like I said, we're going on an adventure," he said, his voice low. "You and me."

"What are you talking about?" I said.

"George got a hot tip on some poachers operating up north. Mostly, they steal pythons, but skinks and birds, too."

"So what does that have to do with *us*?" I asked, taking another big bite of steak. I still wasn't full.

"We're going to do old George a favor," said Ian. "Every poacher in Australia knows him by now, so it's hard for him to investigate undercover."

"So?" I asked.

"So we're going to be his spies. We're going to help him find those rotten blokes and stop them."

A hunk of steak caught in my throat. I coughed it up. "You and *me?*" I said. I shook my head. "Thanks, but no thanks. Too dangerous. Besides, I don't know anything about tracking poachers. I'm a kid. So are you."

"That's the point, Hannah," Ian said. "We're kids. We look perfectly innocent. And you look like a tourist. No one will guess we're helping George investigate."

"No, no, no," I said. Then I said it again. "No."

"We've wanted to nail these smugglers for years," Ian continued, ignoring my "no"s. "We can't do it alone. The other night I asked for someone to come our way to help us."

"And I showed up," I said.

Ian nodded. "Out of nowhere."

"So you think I was sent here to help George

track python poachers?" I whispered, remembering the mission thing.

"Sure I do," said Ian.

"I'm not a tracker," I said flatly.

"No worries, mate," said Ian. "George will do the tracking. We'll just be spying around for information. We can help him locate the smugglers. Then he can go in and arrest them."

"Uh, shouldn't we let the authorities handle this?" I asked, gulping.

Just then, George came back to the table. "Let the authorities handle *what*?" he asked.

"Handle...tracking poachers," I said, looking at Ian. I hoped I wasn't giving away his plan.

"I *am* 'the authorities,'" said George. "I'm a wildlife officer." He pulled out a card with his photo on it.

I examined the card to make sure it wasn't fake. Not that I'd know the difference. But it looked official, with a government stamp and all.

"George's nickname is 'Skinkman,'" Ian said proudly. "He slinks around the bush like a skink, and sneaks up on poachers."

I handed George his card back, nodding as if I approved.

"So how do the poachers capture the animals?" I asked. "Especially the dangerous ones?"

"They put them to sleep with drugs and stuff them in bags, boxes, whatever," Ian said.

"Then they ship them out of the country and sell them?" I asked.

"Yeah," Ian answered. "By boat or plane, from secret hiding places."

Tiny came over to our booth and took my plate away. I'd ended up inhaling that whole steak in no time flat. I guess traveling thousands of miles in a few seconds really takes it out of you.

Just then, at that very moment, I got another mysterious message! I was looking at the menu, in case I needed to sample an Australian dessert, and the weirdest thing happened. On the menu, the letters of: "Try Our Latest Cheesecake—It's Delicious!" started to go fuzzy, then clear, then fuzzy again. When they finally cleared for good, they spelled out: "There Is Life in the Coffins—of the Dead!"

TINY'S MENU

TRY OUR LATEST CHEESECAKE— IT'S DELICIOUS!

I gasped.

"Hannah, what's wrong? You look like you just saw a ghost," said Ian.

But I knew it wasn't any ghost. It was another message from Aurora!

Chapter 6

Meeting an Angel

"Excuse me," I said, getting up from the booth. "I'm going to the bathroom."

I had no idea where I'd find Aurora. But I knew she was around somewhere, waiting for me.

I scooted out the back door, following the arrows that said WOMEN'S ROOM. They pointed me around back, by the parking lot.

I glanced over my shoulder to the right, then to the left, squinting my eyes like a sneaky criminal. No angel. A few truckers were hanging out in the parking lot, but they didn't pay any attention to me.

"So what did that 'coffin' message mean?" I said out loud.

No answer.

"Aurora?" I called, getting a little impatient now.

I looked around for an angel sign—a cloud or a feather or something. The only sign was the one on the bathroom door that said OMEN. Somebody had scratched off the W. That was no angel sign, I hoped.

Finally, I heard a voice. But it wasn't Aurora's.

"Don't look in a usual boneyard," it said.

This voice wasn't sweet, like Aurora's voice. It was younger, and bossy.

"Who are you?" I demanded, being bossy right back.

"My name is Demetriel," the voice answered, clear as a bell. "But you may call me Demi."

"I have *two* angels?" I said, frowning.

"At least," Demi answered. "To tell you the truth, Hannah, you need as much help as you can get. You're not exactly a piece of cake to protect, you know. Most kids are easy. They just go from home to school to—"

"Okay, okay," I cut her off. I hate being told I'm different. Ms. Crybaby says stuff like that about me all the time. So I'm an adventurous person. I was also in a hurry right now. "So what exactly was that message on the menu supposed to mean?"

I listened for Demi's answer. Nothing.

I wondered if I'd made Demi mad. I was new at this angel thing. Maybe I scared her off.

"Hello? Are you there?" I called.

Out of the corner of my eye, I could see the truckers staring at me from the other side of the parking lot. I must have been too loud. I ducked into the OMEN room and stood by the sink.

"Demi?" I whispered. "Sorry."

I swear I felt a tug on my hair. "Ow!" I looked in the mirror. Sure enough, a few strands were sticking up all over the place.

me looking in the mirror

"Look," Demi said, rather cool now. "I work hard to protect you. I suppose I'm pretty much what you'd call your guardian angel. I used to watch you fly in your crib."

I got a chill up and down my arms. "You did?" I said. I wondered what *else* she knew about me.

"I know plenty about you, Hannah Martin," she replied, reading my mind. "So the least you can do is *listen* when I talk to you."

"Okay. Sorry. You're right," I said quickly. "So translate for me—coffins and boneyards? You're talking about a cemetery, right? And what exactly is it we're looking for, anyway?"

"It's *my* job to give messages and *your* job to figure them out," Demi replied. "If I told you everything, you'd never learn to think for yourself."

This was crazy. "Come on. Help me out here.

Just a hint?" I begged. The bathroom door swung open and a lady came in. I didn't want her to hear me talking to myself, so I went back outside.

"Demi?" I whispered, hoping she had followed me out.

She had. "It would be a grave mistake to look in a cemetery," she said, chuckling. "Perhaps you should ask your young Australian friend. He knows a lot of things that you don't. He will help you."

"Okay," I said with a sigh. The lady from the bathroom came out and gave me a funny look, then walked past me.

I turned around to go back to Tiny's, but a man was standing in front of me, blocking my way. One look at him, and my whole body went cold. He towered over me, and when the sunlight hit his eyes, they shimmered like gold.

I took a small step to the side. The tall man didn't budge. By now the truckers had left the parking lot, the bathroom lady had left, and there wasn't a soul in sight.

I was trapped!

Chapter 7

On Our Own

I backed away from the tall, golden-eyed man, pretending to wave to a friend. I don't think I fooled him. Then I headed quickly across the parking lot before he could grab me. When I felt safer, I tried to walk slowly—normally—so he wouldn't know how scared I was.

When I got inside the cafe, Ian and George were gone! I panicked, my heart pounding. If the golden-eyed man was still here, and George and Ian had left…?

Tiny caught my eye and signaled toward the door. "They're waiting for you, mate," he said.

I rushed out the door and headed toward the Jeep, which was parked just outside.

"What's wrong?" said Ian, looking alarmed.

"Nothing," I said. "I just got scared by some guy."

Ian jumped down from the Jeep, ready for a fight. "Where is he? What did he do to you, Hannah?"

I grabbed him by the wrist and pulled him back. The golden-eyed man was nowhere in sight. "Nothing happened, Ian," I said. "It was just some guy on his way to the men's room, I guess. He looked scary to me, that's all."

"You can't be too careful when you're traveling with a tracker," Ian said. "You never know what dangerous blokes George has on his back."

"You two mates wait here," said George, frowning.

He went back inside Tiny's and came back a few minutes later. "I think we're all right," he said. "I didn't spot anybody suspicious. But we'll be on guard just the same."

He started the Jeep and we headed north.

"You looked as if somebody pointed a bone at you back there, Hannah," said George.

Ian laughed.

"What do you mean, 'pointed a bone'?" I asked, confused.

"It's an aboriginal punishment," Ian said. "Maybe George can explain."

"It's when a medicine man sings and chants while he points a bone right at you," said George.

"That's all?" I asked. It didn't sound like too awful a punishment to me.

"Yeah, that's all...until you

pointing a bone

die," Ian said. "Sometimes you die instantly. Sometimes it takes a few months."

I shuddered, picturing the golden-eyed man pointing a bone at me when nobody was looking. "Is it like an evil spell?" I asked.

"Not exactly," George answered. "It has to do with our law. Bone-pointing is done only to people who continue their evil ways even after they've been warned many times to stop."

"The only way to save your life is to go to a more powerful medicine man," Ian added. "Sometimes if you're lucky, he can reverse the bone-pointing."

For some reason, I knew they weren't pulling my leg. Bone-pointing was one of those things David would probably say was hogwash, like flying with your feet on the ground. I tend to believe in those kinds of things. Just because it's never happened to you doesn't mean it's not real. Anyway, I was glad to be on the road, getting farther and farther away from that creepy man.

During the drive I thought about how amazing it was to have two angels: Aurora, my star-and-cloud angel, and Demetriel, my bossy guardian angel. I really did think they'd sent me here. Don't ask me how they did it, though.

I also thought about the coffin clue. Maybe it wasn't just a coincidence that George had mentioned bone-pointing right after I got the bone-and-coffin messages. Was I onto something? I opened my journal and started a new section, "Clues and Messages":

> "There is life in the coffins of the dead."
> "Don't look in a usual boneyard."
> Bone-pointing

It felt like hours passed. The road wound out of the desert, through the mountains, then into an area with green grass and trees. The best part was when we passed a bunch of kangaroos hopping along. I was so excited.

"Isn't it convenient that kangaroos carry their babies in their pouches?" I asked. "Don't you wish people had pouches?"

George and Ian didn't seem to think my question was worth answering. I guess they see a ton of kangaroos all the time, so they're probably tired of thinking about these things.

When we finally stopped, we were still in the middle of nowhere. I figured Ian and I were getting out. But it was George who hauled out his bag and left.

"Good luck, mate," Ian called after him. "Go get 'em!"

George turned and gave us a thumbs-up. Then we watched him walk into the trees, and he disappeared. I imagined him turning into "Skinkman," slithering around unseen, then suddenly pouncing on a bunch of surprised poachers.

Skinkman

But where did that leave Ian and me?

I turned to Ian. "So we're on our own now," I said. My stomach felt jumpy.

"No worries, mate," Ian said. "We'll see old George again soon enough."

He hopped behind the wheel of the Jeep.

"Are you old enough to drive this thing?" I asked.

"Not in big towns like Sydney or Canberra," Ian answered. "But here in the Outback, I've been driving since I was ten. Out here a bloke needs wheels, mate."

Things were definitely different here in the Outback. Oh, well. I had enough to worry about right now, like angels and poachers and stolen pythons—and finding a phone that worked.

Ian told me that George had been tracking poachers forever. "He's from the Larrakeyah tribe, who live up this way at Humpty Doo. This is sacred land to them. All the plants and animals that live on it are sacred, too."

George, Ian went on, could never work in an office. He had to be outside, where he could be near the trees and the earth and the animals. George despised poaching, and he vowed never to give up until every last poacher had been caught. The ones George was after right now had been operating for years.

Ian drove a few miles, then slowed down and pulled the Jeep off the road.

"We're here already?" I asked. Whatever "here" meant.

Ian nodded. "Our first investigative stop," he said. "We'll hang out at the market, grab a bite to eat, pretend to shop. You get the idea. With a bit of luck, we'll pick up a clue or two."

Shopping and eating and hanging out sounded like visiting a mall to me. Very refreshing after being in the bush all night and all day. Maybe I could use a few of my twenty Australian dollars to buy something. And maybe there'd be a phone. But when I got out of the Jeep and looked around, all I saw was a sort of giant yard sale going on.

"That's the market," Ian said.

So much for all my big mall plans.

THE OPEN-AIR MARKET

"Sometimes people sell illegal goods here, like endangered animals," Ian continued. "Or they take illegal orders and meet the customers later in a secret place."

"So do we watch for people selling pythons?" I asked.

"It's not that obvious," Ian said. "Just stay alert, maybe eavesdrop on a few conversations."

Later I bought a vest just like this and a pair of shorts. It was hot, hot, HOT in the North!

PYTHONS ON SALE
ONE DAY ONLY

Before we went spying around, I had to tell Ian about the clue on Tiny's menu. *Ask your Australian friend,* Demi had said. I wasn't sure how to bring the subject up, without Ian thinking I was a total lunatic.

Ian, I got a message from this angel, you see... No, that sounded a little nuts.

Ian, the menu back at Tiny's didn't really say "cheesecake." It said "coffin"... No, that wouldn't work either.

I'd have to discuss this whole thing in a simpler way.

"Ian, is it possible the poachers are operating out of a graveyard of some kind?"

He raised his eyebrows.

"Well, not exactly a cemetery," I rushed on, remembering Demi's warning about grave mistakes. "A place with coffins."

"Why do you say that?" Ian asked, glancing around. It seemed like we were always doing that, checking for danger.

"There is life in the coffins of the dead," I quoted. "Does that mean anything to you?"

Ian rubbed his chin, thinking. "Hmm. Life in the coffins...like dead people who are still alive. What about the burial ground near Alligator Bay? People say the place is haunted."

A haunted burial ground? Yikes! Half of me was scared, the other half excited.

"It's not a regular cemetery, is it?" I asked anxiously. Probably not, if it was haunted. Was that what Demi had meant?

"There aren't any headstones or anything, just a lot of bones covered with dirt." Ian sounded hesitant. "I'm not sure we should go there, Hannah."

"Why not?" I asked.

"Well," Ian said slowly, "they say, on certain nights, the dead get up from their graves and walk around."

I shivered.

"But the place *is* right on the water," Ian said. "A perfect place for shipping illegal goods."

"Maybe we should check it out," I said. (That's not exactly true. Actually, I said that we absolutely, positively *had* to check it out.)

Ian thought it over. Finally, he nodded.

"Okay. We'll head up that way when we're done here at the market," he said.

"Great!" I exclaimed. I could feel my blood rushing through me. This was really getting exciting.

"We'll need to split up," Ian said. "That way, we'll cover the area faster. Just watch for clues as you wander around the marketplace."

I grabbed my pen and journal from my knapsack, ready for action. Ian snatched them right out of my hand.

"Hide those, Hannah!" he said. "You're supposed to be a *tourist,* not a newspaper reporter!"

"But I keep track of everything in my journal!" I protested, grabbing my stuff right back. You have no idea how mad I get when somebody tries to confiscate my journal. Ms. Crybaby does it all the time when she thinks I'm not paying attention. She might as well try to reach in and rip my heart out.

"What if I just draw a few pictures? Don't tourists do that?"

"Suit yourself," Ian said, shrugging. "Just don't look too conspicuous."

I ripped the "Clues and Messages" page out of my journal and folded it in my pocket. I stuffed my journal under the seat of the Jeep.

"Try to look like you're having fun, not like you're spying," Ian told me. Then he and I went off in different directions.

I could do that.

The first fun I had was watching artists paint on big, dry pieces of bark. They painted things they saw around them: snakes and skinks, trees and cockatoos. After the bark paintings, I tried throwing a curved piece of wood called a boomerang. It's kind of like an Australian Frisbee. And it actually worked! It flew through the air and came right back to me!

boomerang

BARK PAINTINGS
They're painted with
tiny, tiny dots

I was having fun, all right, but I was also coming up empty-handed on the investigation. No clues. No suspicious meetings. No pythons for sale.

So I went on, looking for more fun. I stopped by a group of musicians who were playing some really cool-looking instruments. I've always loved to touch things. In stores back home, it drives salespeople crazy. But these musicians didn't mind at all when I touched their instruments. I'd never seen anything like them before, at least not in the Kennedy Middle School Band.

"What are these?" I asked, picking up two sticks made of smooth wood.

"They're called bilma sticks, mate," one of the musicians told me. "Try them."

There was a fat lizard carved on one, and a bird with a long beak on the other.

bilma sticks

"How do I do it?" I asked.

He showed me, drumming a bilma stick on his didgeridoo as he played it. I picked up one of the didgeridoos and I hummed and *pffftt*ted into it. A tiny sound came out! I was so proud—I was getting better all the time! Then I started drumming with a bilma stick while I played. That was a challenge, all right. It was kind of like rubbing your stomach and patting your head at the same time.

didgeridoos

I was really getting into it now. The other musicians were playing that strange buzzing music. All of the notes mixed in my head with the ancient moon music I'd heard back in class.

Suddenly, I felt a slow shiver make its way up

my spine. My skin got all crawly, like that feeling you get when someone is watching you. I glanced around the market and caught a glimpse of a tall figure under a tree. I squinted until I could make out the face.

It was the golden-eyed man, staring right back at me!

Chapter 8

The Women Who Turned into Stars

I jumped to my feet, dropping the didgeridoo into the lap of the musician sitting next to me. "Sorry," I said quickly. Then I looked back toward the tree where the man was standing. He was gone!

I took off like a shot. I raced through the marketplace, past carvings and paintings, boots and boomerangs, searching for Ian. I finally found him at a booth where they sold cowboy hats. I must have looked panicky, because he shot me a stern look.

"Hannah!" he called loudly. "Help me pick out a souvenir for my dad!"

I was anxious to tell Ian about the golden-eyed man, right that very minute, but I knew he wanted me to play the tourist game. I went along with our plan.

"Here's a good one," I said, putting a cowboy

hat on my head. It was brown leather, with a thin dark band. I whirled in a circle, modeling it.

"Good choice!" Ian said. "It'll be perfect for Dad." He paid the man for the hat and whispered to me, "You just got yourself an Aussie souvenir, mate."

I checked out my new look in the mirror. I must say, the hat made me look very adventurous. I felt like I should have a live rattlesnake in one hand and a boomerang in the other.

Ian cocked his head, sizing me up. "It suits you, Hannah," he said.

"Thanks, mate," I replied, grinning. Then I tugged him by the sleeve of his shirt and led him to a quiet corner.

"I saw him again," I whispered. "That creepy-looking man. The one from Tiny's. He's here."

"This is not good," said Ian, frowning. "What does he look like?"

"He's very tall, and he's wearing a blue denim vest," I answered, recalling what I could. "He has dark skin, and sort of golden eyes."

Ian looked confused. "What do you mean, 'golden eyes'?" he asked.

"I mean just that. They're gold," I insisted. "I know it sounds strange, but when the sun hits them, that's what color they are."

Ian still didn't seem to know what to make of

that. "Let's see if we can track him down," he said.

We searched the whole market but didn't see a trace of Golden Eyes. Now I started to wonder. Had I really seen him here? Or was I just imagining things?

As we passed by one of the artists, a painting caught my attention. I don't know why, I just had to stare at it. It was made out of hundreds of little dots. The artist was sitting on the ground next to it, painting a new work. He was using a stick, dabbing one dot at a time onto the canvas.

I pulled my journal page from my pocket and pretended to draw the artist. Actually, I was drawing a sketch of his painting. It looked like this:

I couldn't believe it. See how the dots form a didgeridoo? Only it was wider than a real didgeridoo. And I was sure the drawing on it was a rattlesnake.

"We'd better get a move on, Hannah," Ian called from the next booth.

I walked over to him, still finishing up my sketch.

"What have you got there?" he asked.

"Something about this painting is important," I said. "I don't know why."

Ian examined my sketch. "Hmm…a rattler on a didgeridoo?" he said slowly. "I'm not sure about that. Well, hold on to it. If we're going to get to the burial ground, we'd better head out. It'll be dark soon."

The idea of visiting the burial ground in the dark was not appealing to me at all, but we got into the Jeep and were soon back on the road.

On the way to Alligator Bay, Ian told me a lot of stuff. He said there was an aboriginal story for every single living creature on earth—birds and skinks, pythons and kangaroos. He told me one about how these women eating yams flew into the sky and turned into stars. When it started to get dark (we were still nowhere near the burial ground), Ian showed me the cluster of star-women. Sure enough, there they were, twinkling away, right where the story said they had landed.

"Where did you learn that story?" I asked. It was the strangest, most magical story I'd ever heard. I mean, *yams*?

"From George," he told me. "George is full of stories. Okay, Hannah, it's your turn. Now *you* tell a story."

"I don't know any," I said.

Ian turned and frowned at me. "Everybody has stories," he said. "Just tell me something that really happened in your life. Something that didn't happen to me, because I wasn't there."

That made sense, I guess. I decided to tell him about this substitute teacher, Ms. Montgomery,

Ms. Montgomery

who comes in when Ms. Crybaby is sick. When we studied mythology, she dashed around the classroom at eight-thirty in the morning, acting out the lives of the Greek gods. She has wild curly black hair, and she starts class before the first bell even rings because she's so excited about whatever we'll be learning that day. We straggle into class half-asleep, but she always comes over and yells in your ear if you start to doze off.

"Today is a brand-new day!" she announces. "Don't let another minute of it go by with your eyes closed! You'll never know what you missed!"

I looked over at Ian to see if my story was dull compared to the yam stars.

"This is great," he assured me. "I like hearing about Ms. Montgomery."

So then I told him about how she was Icarus one day, flying all around our desks, with her arms outstretched like wings. But then the wings began to melt because Icarus flew too close to the sun, even though he'd been warned ahead of time not to do it. Ms. Montgomery got all dramatic, crashing to the floor as her "wings" dripped away tragically. The whole class sat stunned. I think, for a moment, we really thought she was dead.

"But she wasn't dead?" asked Ian, sounding a little worried.

"Of course not!" I said. "She's just a good actress."

It was pitch-dark by the time we arrived at Alligator Bay. All I could see was empty blackness, and lots of stars, and the moon shining on the water. It was absolutely, totally silent. Much more silent than the Outback. No howling dingoes, for one thing.

"Maybe we should wait until dawn to go exploring," said Ian, stopping the Jeep.

I agreed. I really, seriously did *not* want to go snooping around a burial ground in the pitch-dark, tripping over dead people's bones.

Ian got a fire going, and we had some tucker. (How do you like my Aussie talk?) He made us lamb stew and potatoes, which he'd gotten at the marketplace. I cut the onions and cried the whole time.

"We need to take turns keeping watch," Ian said. "If there's a shipment out of here tonight, we can't have the smugglers find us asleep."

"Tell me what these poachers look like," I said. "How will I know one when I see one?" I still had this boiled-egg picture in my brain, as if poachers

would have bloated faces and veins
full of cholesterol. Gross.

eggs = poachers

"They look normal, like any
bloke on the street," Ian said.
"You'll know who they are when you see 'em in
action."

"Of course, *we're* not going to try and stop
them," I said. "Right?"

"Right," he answered. "That's George's job.
Remember, we're just spying for clues."

I agreed to take the first shift. Ian moved the
Jeep behind a grove of ghost gum trees. He
pitched his swag so it was hidden between the
Jeep and the trees.

"Wake me at one o'clock," he said. "And good
luck."

The whole four hours I was on duty, my imag-
ination ran wild. Everything that rustled in the
breeze sounded like a dead body rising from a
grave. I kept thinking I heard footsteps approach-
ing. Then I imagined I saw gold eyes glittering
between the ghost gum trees. *Where are my angels
now?* I wondered.

The truth is, nothing happened. Or maybe the
angels *were* there, silently protecting me. By the
end of my shift, I was fading into sleep.

"Ian!" I called softly. It was one o'clock on the
dot, and his turn. "Time to get up!"

He was up and in the Jeep beside me in a split
second.

"Anything suspicious?" he asked.

"Not a thing," I said. "It's quiet as a cemetery around here."

"Not funny, Hannah," he told me.

I wanted to sleep in the Jeep, but the seats didn't go back the way they do in our minivan at home. I got out and wrapped myself up in the swag.

Let me tell you, it is impossible to get a restful sleep when you're lying ten feet away from a bunch of buried dead people. I dreamed about Katie and David. They were searching a haunted house. Suddenly the floor gave out below them and swallowed them up. They got sucked down into a coffin. It was horrible. Terrible. The worst. They were screaming bloody murder, and nobody was there to help them. The whole place was bustling with skeletons, bony dead people rattling around, laughing at them.

How could I have known then that my dream was a warning?

(I always put clouds around my dream pictures
so I remember they were dreams)

Chapter 9

Don't Dig Your Own Grave

I woke up in a sweat. Ian had started a fire, and the sky over the bay looked gray and stormy.

"So we go bone-exploring today," he said cheerfully.

"Yep," I said, crawling out of the swag. I didn't exactly feel perky. I was sleepy and sweaty, and I think my teeth had grown fuzz from not brushing for two days.

"What exactly do you think we're looking for here, Ian?" I asked.

"Any signs that poachers have been around," he answered. "Bird feathers, snake skins, footprints—that sort of thing."

Just then, we felt a sprinkle of rain.

"Better get out your rain gear," Ian said. "The sky is about to open up." He ran to the Jeep and took out an army-green poncho.

I followed him and pulled out my yellow rain jacket and boots. I also put on my new hat and slid my pack onto my back. I was all set.

Ready for the rain!

"You know, Hannah," said Ian, looking at the sky again, "it might be better to wait out the storm and try later. We're going to have a major downpour."

In case you haven't noticed, I'm not the most patient person in the world. I was ready to go right then, rain or no rain.

"Let's just look around until the rain gets bad," I said.

Ian shrugged. "In that case, you'd better leave the hat," he said. "You'll lose it in the storm."

I tossed the hat back in the Jeep.

Since we didn't have much time, we decided to separate. The burial grounds were flat, with big mounds of bumpy dirt. The whole area was bordered by trees, except for along the coast.

It was starting to rain harder now.

"You take the east side," Ian instructed. "Walk every square centimeter, and pick up anything the least bit suspicious. I'll take the west section." Sometimes Ian could be kind of bossy.

I started along the tree line, prowling the ground inch by inch. If there'd been any footprints, they'd already been washed away by the rain. It was coming down harder by the minute. Ian had told me the wet season in Australia brings torrential rainstorms that turn into floods. He said there's even a lake that rains fish. The lake completely dries up for years, and then so much rain falls at one time that the fish eggs hatch. Pretty cool, huh? Anyway, from the way things were looking, I'd say the wet season was definitely here.

The first thing I saw was a feather on the ground. It was black and pretty long. I picked it up and tucked it in my pocket, just in case it was a clue. Every once in a while, I thought I saw something important, but they kept turning out to be sticks or stones.

Now it was *really* raining cats and dogs, as Grandma Zoe would say. It was getting more and more difficult to see anything. My boots squished in the dirt, picking up clumps of mud on the soles. Pretty soon I was lumbering around like I had Frankenstein feet.

I stepped onto a nice-looking grassy patch to rub off the mud. The grass turned out to be mixed with green leaves and branches. For some reason, the ground underneath felt funny. It seemed a little shaky, sort of like the thin ice you sometimes hit when you're skating. I carefully scraped one foot on a branch. Suddenly the ground gave way. It collapsed right under me!

I tumbled down into a huge hole. The rain kept pouring in, soaking the mud around me. I scrambled to my feet and found that the hole was deeper than I was tall. I immediately tried digging my fingers into the side to climb out. But hunks of wet mud slid out from under my grasp. I crashed back down into the hole.

I sat for a minute at the bottom, head to toe in muddy slop. Why would this stupid hole have been here, anyway? Then it struck me. This wasn't just any hole. This was a *grave!* It was about six feet deep and the perfect width to hold a body. I sprang to my feet in horror and began to claw wildly, trying to get out.

"Ian!" I screamed. "Help! *Help!!!*"

The rain was crashing down in torrents now. I could barely hear my own voice. Mud was packed under my fingernails and sloshing around in my boots. I hollered at the top of my lungs.

"Help me, Ian! I'm in trouble!"

A voice answered, "Calm down. I'm right here." It was Demetriel.

"Demi, help me!" I screamed. By now, I was knee-deep in a puddle at the bottom of the grave. And I was sinking fast.

"Will you stop flailing around?" Demetriel said, sounding annoyed.

"I can't!" I yelled back. "I'm *stuck* in here!"

"If you calm down, you'll find the way out," she said.

Well, it was easy for *her* to be calm—*she* was an angel. And *she* wasn't getting buried alive!

"Panic won't help, Hannah," Demi said. "If you keep struggling like that, you'll dig your own grave."

"*What are you talking about?*" I yelled. "*I* didn't dig this grave, and *I* did not put myself in here!"

"Well, I told you not to look in a boneyard," Demi said. "I'd sure call this a boneyard. And I did say it would be a grave mistake. Please don't keep putting yourself into so much danger, Hannah. It's unnecessary."

"But I misunderstood you," I moaned. "I thought..."

"Next time, *listen* to what I tell you," she said, cutting me off. "Really listen. And by the way, Hannah, you *can* get yourself out."

I stopped flailing around for a minute and took a few breaths.

"Show me how, Demi," I begged. "Please!"

"Look around you," she said. "You have everything you need to escape."

I didn't need angel lectures right now. I just needed to be pulled out of this hole.

"You're going to leave me here, aren't you?" I whimpered. "You have no intention of saving me. Some guardian angel *you* are."

"Maybe I can't save you, Hannah," she said quietly. "Maybe angels don't have that kind of power."

Suddenly, I felt very alone. I knew Demi was gone.

I started to cry. (I hate it when I do that.)

I was all by myself, deep in a muddy grave, and I didn't know how to get out.

Chapter 10

Back in a Flash

Now I was beyond terrified. My arms and legs were trembling from exhaustion, and the rain was pounding my skin hard, like hail. I knew I'd have to do what Demi told me. I'd have to calm down so I could think.

I covered my face with my hands and squinted through two fingers. On the far side of the grave, I saw a tree branch that was bent over from the rain. Maybe I could just reach it. It was my only chance.

I tried to move my right foot. It sucked up out of the mud and I set it down, just a few inches forward. Then I did the same thing with my left foot. Taking small, careful steps, I slowly made my way across the grave.

I reached for the tree branch. No way. It was at least two feet beyond my reach. I tried jumping up to grab it. No way again. Every time I jumped, I landed deeper in the mud. It was just like Demi had said. I was digging my own grave, deeper and deeper by the minute.

Then a wonderful thought struck me. I had my backpack! I hadn't really checked what was in it yet. I stood very still, so I wouldn't sink any farther, and slipped the pack off my back. No surprise—everything inside was sopping wet.

The flashlight was not going to help me. Neither would the map. And it wasn't exactly a convenient time to figure things out by writing in my now-soggy journal.

I fumbled through the pack, until I discovered a rope. *Yes!* I hauled it out. It was long, all right. Plenty long. It would reach the tree limb.

I put my pack back on and unwound the rope. Still standing very still, I tossed the end up over the limb. Perfect! I pulled down on the short end until both ends of the rope were in my grasp. Then I wrapped them around my hands.

"Here goes!" I said out loud.

Holding on tight, I planted one foot in the mud on the side of the grave. Foot by foot, I slowly trudged up the side, winding the rope around my hands as I went. The mud gave out every now and then, but I kept a fierce grip on the rope, even though it was giving me major burns on my hands. Finally, I had only one more step to go. I planted my knee on top of solid ground and pulled myself up.

I had done it! I was out! *Out!!!* The rain pounded onto my face, but I didn't care.

"Ian!" I yelled. This time he heard me. I could just make him out behind me in the rain.

I ran toward the Jeep, lumbering like Frankenstein the whole way. Ian followed. He was moving a lot slower than I was. That's probably because he hadn't just narrowly escaped live burial.

"Ian!" I yelled as I ran. "We're *leaving now!*"

Back in the Jeep, I started shivering like crazy from the cold and the wet and the close call I'd just had. I wound the rope back into my pack, in case I needed it again, and pulled off my soggy boots and socks. Then I told Ian the whole story.

He was pretty amazed. And scared for me, too. I told him that this boneyard was definitely not the right place to look. Of course, I didn't tell him any details about the message back in Tiny's parking lot bathroom. I didn't say a word about Demi and how she's an angel and all.

Neither of us knew what to do next. We were stumped. The only thing we knew for sure was that we had to get in out of the rain—soon, before we got totally drowned. We drove into the nearest town and headed straight to a restaurant for hot chocolate. Well, *I* had hot chocolate. (They call it "drinking chocolate" here.) Ian had tea. I guess it's an Aussie thing.

We were both very quiet. We stared out at the street, watching the raindrops drip down the window. Ian was acting a little distant. I think he was upset with me.

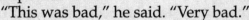

"This was bad," he said. "Very bad."

"Yes," I said.

"It was stupid for us to go out in that wet," he went on. "If George found out what happened to you, he'd be ticked."

"Probably," I agreed.

"We have to be more careful from now on."

"Right," I said.

Suddenly, I felt a terrible pang of loneliness for home. I missed my parents. I missed my dog. I even missed school. And I missed Katie, too. I wanted to tell her about this whole ordeal. I knew she was probably the only person who'd believe me. She'd want to hear every last detail about my adventure. I wanted to be back home. I wanted to be back so badly, it hurt.

I jumped up. "I've got to call my parents," I said.

Ian gave me some coins and told me how to dial the United States. You

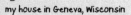

my house in Geneva, Wisconsin

have to plug in a country code before the area code and all. I found a phone at the back of the restaurant and dialed the fifteen numbers. Wouldn't you know it? The answering machine picked up. I heard my own voice say, "Hello. This is the Martin residence. Please leave a message and we'll call you back."

I had no idea what time it was. My parents must have been at work. I'd have to leave a message. I was waiting for the beep when, all of a sudden, I heard a strange noise. It was the same rustling wind sound I'd heard in the didgeridoo yesterday afternoon.

"Hush-sh-sh," it said, like a warm breeze blowing through me. "Hush-sh-sh."

Right at that moment, an incredible, amazing thing happened. I was back in music class! Jimmy Fudge had his same skunk hair, and he was making his power fist. Ms. Crybaby was sniffling, and everything was totally, exactly the same! Not one single second had passed!

I had my flute in my hands, and Katie was looking at me, rolling her eyes to the sky, as if to say, "Can you believe this stupid class?"

Nobody had even noticed that I'd left. Maybe I *hadn't* left. Maybe I'd had some kind of geographic seizure, if there was such a thing. Like your brain checks out of one place and into another. Maybe it's a sort of rare and dangerous disease of the medulla oblongata or something.

I'll have to ask David—he's a walking encyclopedia of bizarre facts. Anyway, the only thing that seemed to have changed was that I was never so happy in all my life to see Jimmy Fudge.

The whole scene was feeling so familiar—but then, in a split second, I was back in Australia again! The phone was in my hand and Ian was still at the table, staring out at the raindrops as if nothing had happened. *What is this?* I wondered. *How can I be in two places at once, having weird adventures in one place, while no time passes in the other?* It was too complicated for me to figure out. It had to be some kind of angel thing.

I hung up the phone and went back to the table. I felt a little cold, so I wrapped my hands around the warm cup of cocoa.

"Everybody's fine?" Ian asked.

"Fine," I said.

I was sorry I didn't get to talk to my parents, but I was also kind of happy. If no time had passed, then nobody at home would be worried about me. That meant I could finish this angel mission thing, and then go back and pick up right where I left off in music class. At least, I *think* that's what it meant.

I was still shivering from the cold and wet, in spite of the cocoa. I reached into my pocket for something to blow my nose and my hand touched a strange object. I pulled it out. It was a rusty old key!

"Where did this come from, Ian?" I asked, totally puzzled.

"No idea, mate," he said. He took the key from me and toyed with it, spinning it around his fingertips.

"I've never seen it before in my life," I said.

"Interesting," Ian said. "It looks very, very old."

"Almost ancient, don't you think, Ian?"

He leaned forward and gave me a look that David would call skeptical. "Maybe it's a clue, Hannah. Another one of those strange messages you seem to be receiving out of nowhere, perhaps."

I didn't appreciate the tone in Ian's voice. He was being skeptical, all right.

"I don't know," I said. I took the key back and tucked it into my pocket again. I was not going to discuss my angels with him, that's for sure.

But I knew he was right. The key was definitely an angel message. Maybe Demi or Aurora had slipped it into my pocket while I was traveling from Australia to home and back again.

I wonder which angel gave me the key

Somehow, that thought made me feel better.

Chapter 11

Temper Tantrums

"Now what?" I asked Ian.

"Back to square one, mate," he said. "And no more of your magic messages."

"What do you mean?" I asked, all huffy.

"This time, we'll go on *my* information, not *yours*."

Did I detect a tiny bit of sarcasm in his voice? I believe I did.

"Hannah, your little bone-and-coffin adventure nearly got you killed," Ian went on. "I suggest we follow the facts *I* know from George."

"Oh, excu-u-u-se me for trying to help," I said.

"Don't overreact, Hannah," Ian said, taking a loud slurp of tea. That did it. I was furious! It took everything in me to keep from reaching across the table to strangle him.

"Look, I didn't ask for this big adventure, you know!" I exploded. "Do you think I really *want* to be here, getting covered in mud, catching pneumonia from the rain, tracking some stupid snakes and animals I don't even care about?"

"You don't *care* about them?" Ian repeated, raising his eyebrows. He looked kind of hurt.

I always do that. I always say things I don't really mean when I'm mad. But by the time the words come out, I'm so caught up in being mad that I can't turn back.

"That's right, I don't care," I said. "This is all so stupid, I'd rather be at—at *school!*" Then I got even more carried away. "I'd rather even be in *history* class. So there!" That was as low as I could think of getting at that moment.

"Fine," Ian said quietly, taking out his wallet to pay the bill.

"And you're not paying for my hot chocolate!" I added. "I can do that myself, thank you very much!"

"Sure. I'll see you around, Hannah. Enjoy your history class." With that, Ian got up, put the cash for his tea on the table, and left the restaurant.

I just sat there, seething. I was still shivering, too. I kept feeling hot, then cold, then hot. *Good,* I thought. *I'll go home!*

I closed my eyes and sent a message to Demetriel.

"Send me back," I told her. "Send me back to music class again."

Nothing happened. I guess I wasn't making a connection.

"Please," I tried. Maybe I hadn't been polite enough. After all, I was talking to an angel. "*Please* send me back."

Nothing.

I paid for my hot chocolate and went outside. It was still raining, but now it was down to a drizzle. I walked until I found a bench. Then I sat down and stared at the sky. It was plain gray, with not a single white cloud in it.

"Aurora," I pleaded. "Send me a sign. *Please*. I want to go back home."

No clouds showed up. No sweet voice came through. I felt doomed.

Of course I cared about the animals George and Ian were trying to save. Especially the pythons. I cared about the parrots, too, and the skinks and the elephants and the gorillas—all of those animals all over the world that were being taken away from their families. Last year in school, I did a science project about endangered species. When I read about the gorillas, I couldn't stop crying.

All these animals were being kidnapped or killed for only one reason: money. In my opinion, that's evil. I pulled out my journal from my knapsack. I listed every evil thing I could think of:

— Stealing animals from their families

— Making money by hurting animals or the earth or other people

— Murder (of course)

— Making fun of what somebody else believes in (like angels)

— Pretending to be somebody's friend and then stabbing them in
the back

I finally ran out of steam on the evil thing. I drew a little picture of my hands around somebody's neck and filled in the face to look like Ian's. Then I closed my journal. I felt better.

When I looked up, I noticed a sign on the building in front of me. It's funny, but I hadn't noticed it before. Maybe I had been too angry at Ian.

ANIMAL PROTECTION AGENCY OF AUSTRALIA, it said. Somehow, I wasn't surprised. I figured I might as well stop in. It looked as if the angels weren't going to send me home until I finished this mission. And I could do it *my* way, angel messages and all, without Ian criticizing me.

I walked over and went into the building. It turned out to be a tiny office, but that made sense. It wasn't like it was in a big city or anything. I guess they didn't need a lot of computers and fax machines and stuff to track down poachers.

There were three desks, but the only person in the office was a blond man with a long ponytail and wire-rimmed glasses.

"Good day," he said. It sounded like *G'day*.

"How can I help you?" he asked. His Aussie accent was really strong.

I took a deep breath.

"I'm looking for some information on a certain group of poachers," I began.

The man's eyebrows lifted. "Have a seat," he said. "My name is Miles Carver."

I didn't want to give him my name. What if the poachers got a hold of it somehow? But Mr. Carver didn't ask.

Mr. Carver

"I'm working with some, uh, trackers," I said.

"I see," Mr. Carver said, looking terribly serious. "And what kind of poachers are they—excuse me—are *you* tracking?" I was definitely getting the idea he didn't believe me.

"Well, they would be python poachers," I said.

"The Oenpelli pythons?" he asked.

"Um...yes," I said. The more I talked, the more I realized I didn't know what I was talking about.

Mr. Carver seemed more impressed now. "So you know what an Oenpelli python is, do you?"

Actually, I had no idea what it was. Ian hadn't really talked about specific species of snakes. I happened to glimpse a map of Australia on the wall in back of Mr. Carver. There was a region called Oenpelli that was highlighted. That must be where we were right now.

"Sure. It's a snake from Oenpelli," I said.

Mr. Carver had a hard time keeping his mouth from turning up into a smile.

"Right!" he said encouragingly, like a teacher who wants to hear more facts. "And…?"

I was dead meat. I didn't have a clue what to say next.

"And it's purple and black, and rather short for a python, right?" he prompted.

I nodded.

Mr. Carver chuckled. Then he reached into his desk drawer and pulled out a photo, which he set down on the desk facing me. In the picture was the longest snake I'd ever seen. It was stretched out on a huge rock.

"*This* is an Oenpelli python," he said. "It's about twenty-three feet long, one of the longest snakes on earth."

"And it's not purple and black, is it?" I said. Now I felt really dumb.

Oenpelli python

"No," he said. "It matches its environment. An Oenpelli python actually changes color, in much the same way a chameleon does, for protection. It blends in with its surroundings to hide from its enemies."

"No kidding!" I exclaimed. I was totally fascinated. A snake five times as long as me! And it could change colors, too.

"The Oenpellis were discovered by scientists

only about twenty years ago," Mr. Carver continued. "They live in remote areas of the bush, you see. The aborigines have always known about them, of course. But as soon as scientists announce the existence of a new and particularly rare snake, the poachers begin hunting them for high prices."

The poor Oenpelli pythons! No wonder George and Ian were trying so hard to help them.

Mr. Carver stood up and stared down at me. "And now, young sheila," he said (Sheila? Who was *she*?), "I want you to know that tracking poachers is extremely dangerous business. The Australian government has the situation well under control. You can stop worrying now and enjoy the rest of your visit here Down Under."

I thought I'd gotten steamed with Ian. But now I was getting mad all over again. I hate it when people talk to me like I don't know what I'm doing, just because I'm a kid.

"But I want to help," I said. "I'm already on an undercover job with some other people. I'd like you to give me any information that will help me find where the poachers are working right now."

"'An undercover job,'" Mr. Carver said, trying to hold back that little smile again. "So who, exactly, are you working with?"

"George," I burst out, without thinking. *Oh, no!* I thought. Now I'd really blown it. Some spy *I* was.

"George who?" asked the man.

"Uh...George...um...Skinkman," I answered.

I thought Mr. Carver was going to burst out laughing right in my face.

"Will you wait here just a moment, please?" he said. "I'll be right with you."

He backed through a doorway, chuckling and staring at me as if I were some strange and highly entertaining breed of human. Coming here had not been the best idea.

Mr. Carver was gone for about ten minutes. It seemed like forever. I waited there, wriggling in my chair, still cold and soggy. When Mr. Carver came back, George was with him!

I almost died. What was *he* doing here?

"Hello, Hannah," George said simply. "We can go now."

I felt my face turn bright red.

"Thanks, Miles," George said. "Cheers."

That must be how they say good-bye in Australia.

George led me out the door and down the stairs. I walked behind him in silence, feeling like a fool. What a stupid, stupid thing I had done! I'd blown my cover *and* I'd probably gotten George in a whole bunch of trouble! I'd forgotten he was a wildlife officer.

The silence was unbearable. It was like when your parents find out you've done something bad, and they don't say a word. They just give you the cold treatment while they contemplate your punishment.

There was nothing to do but wait for the bomb to drop.

Chapter 12

♡ ♡=☆(☆♭♭=☆

An Angel Message

I followed George around the back of the building.

"What's going on, Hannah?" he asked.

"I thought…well…I wanted to help you catch
those poachers, and…"

George looked at me in silence, waiting.

"And I guess I got carried away," I finished.

George still didn't say a word.

"I'm sorry if I got you in trouble," I said.

"You didn't get me in trouble, mate," he said.
"But you could get yourself and Ian in a whole
slew of trouble if you keep on jumping into dangerous situations without thinking first."

"I just want to help you and Ian save those
animals," I said lamely. "That's all."

George smiled. "I know you do, Hannah. And
you *can* help. If you come across any information

that you think I can use, let me know. Ian knows how to get a hold of me."

"Great!" I said eagerly.

"Just remember," he added sternly, "you and Ian are *not* the trackers. *I* am."

"Okay," I said. "I promise I'll be more careful. Sorry, George."

"By the way, Hannah, why aren't you with Ian?" George asked.

"We had sort of a disagreement," I explained. "It was all my fault."

"Well, if you're interested, I just happened to spot Ian going into the library, round the corner," George said, pointing.

"Thanks," I said. "And by the way, who's Sheila?"

George smiled. "That's Australian for 'girl,' mate."

As I started off at a jog, George called to me. "Hannah!"

"Yes?" I said.

"Remember, keep your nose clean!"

I think that meant stay out of trouble.

I smiled and nodded and headed toward the library. Before I'd taken five running steps, I felt a tug on my hair again. I hate that.

"Hold on one minute there," Demetriel commanded. I stopped.

"Uh, hi, Demi," I said weakly.

"We have a few rules that we need to go over

before you continue," she said.

"Okay," I said with a sigh. First George, now my guardian angel.

"Rule number one: Do not intentionally put yourself in danger."

I nodded. I'd already gotten the message on *that* one.

She continued with her angel lecture. "Rule number two: Do not put anyone *else* in danger."

I knew that one, too.

"How would you say you've been doing so far, Hannah?" Demi asked.

"Not too well," I admitted.

I felt like I was in the principal's office. Maybe Demi was going to expel me from Australia. And now I didn't want to leave. Not yet, anyway.

"Are you taking me off the mission?" I asked.

"If I could, I would," she answered. "But that's not my decision. Aurora assigns the missions."

Angels had particular jobs? This was news to me.

"You're very brave and very smart, Hannah," Demi went on, smoothing out my hair. "You're also wearing me out. If you give me much more trouble, I'll have to report you to Aurora."

"Okay," I said.

"Use your eyes and ears to help Ian. And your heart. But stay safe. Got it?"

"Got it," I said.

I felt another gentle tug on my hair, and then Demi was gone.

I continued on my way to the library. Ian was in the reference section, paging through a book on top of a big pile of books.

I slid into the chair across from him. He glanced up and gave me a cool look.

"I'm sorry, Ian," I said. "I didn't mean to put us in danger and screw up the mission."

He didn't answer.

"It won't happen again," I added.

He nodded and passed an open book over to me. "I found something interesting," he said. "It's about the black palm cockatoo."

I guess Ian was one of those people who forgive easily. Boy, was I relieved! I really did feel bad about exploding at him.

As I looked at the cockatoo page, Ian started to tell me why he wanted to stop these poachers so much. He said he'd always loved animals, and a lot of the kids in his class thought he went overboard. When he was in fourth grade, some kids were throwing stones at cockatoos. One of them was hurt and couldn't fly anymore. Ian picked it up, took it inside, and mended its wing. He named it Buddy. He taught it to say,

Buddy

"I can fly. I can fly." Then some nasty kid in his class stole the cockatoo from the science class one night. Nobody ever saw Buddy again.

As Ian was telling me the story, his eyes got a little teary. I love boys who can cry. I mean, it's not like I had a crush on Ian or anything. It's just that, well, you know what I mean. I like boys who aren't always being loud and tough like Jimmy Fudge. It's nice when they show their real feelings.

Anyway, I was looking at the information on cockatoos, when I turned the page and *bam!* There was another message, but a very, very weird one. It looked like this:

↑💀⌣♀⁺↑↑⁺⁖♡⌣(⌣💀↑♦ ⌣💀☆

♡⁖↑ ⌣(⁓⌣△♦ ↑💀✋☆ ↑⁖

↑💀⌣♀⁺↑⁺⁖ ♡⌣(♪☆⌣💀↑♦

"Hey, Ian, there's some kind of code here!" I said excitedly.

He leaned over the book, and his eyes shot wide open. "Amazing!" he said. "That wasn't there before."

"Do you think it's some kind of aboriginal language?" I asked. "Or an ancient dreamtime language?" *Or maybe even angel language*, I added to myself.

"Never seen anything like it," Ian said, shrugging. "I don't think it's a real language."

"Let's ask the librarian," I suggested.

When we went over to the information desk, the librarian shook her head, bewildered. "It must be a printing error," she said, pulling a pencil out from behind her ear. She noted the name of the book on a piece of paper. "I'll notify the publisher."

She closed the book and set it on a special shelf below her desk.

"But we need the book back," I said. "Please."

"Oh, of course," she said, pulling it out again. "Just bring it back to me when you've finished."

I could see that Ian was getting a little agitated now. He pulled his spiral notebook out of his pocket.

Seeing him do that, I remembered my journal. And my backpack! There was still some stuff in there I hadn't gotten a good look at. Or maybe stuff just kept appearing when I wasn't looking. The angels again, probably.

I grabbed Ian's sleeve and dragged him into one of those little booths where nobody can disturb you while you study. I turned my backpack upside down and scattered the contents all over the desk.

"Maybe there's something here that will tell us how to decode that message!" I whispered.

"Don't you know what's in your own knapsack?" Ian asked, looking a little disgusted.

I didn't bother to answer.

We tore through the contents. There was still so much stuff I hadn't had time to check out. Most of it was wet. Ian picked up a small leather-bound book that looked like an address book.

"Eureka!" he said as he opened it. He thumped me on the back, with one big, happy thud. "This is it!"

"What? What?" I said, stretching my neck to see what he'd found.

"I think it's a decoder!" he exclaimed, pulling a cardboard disk from inside the little book.

"Show me!" I said. I couldn't stand the suspense.

Ian set the decoder on the desk and sat down. I sat down right next to him.

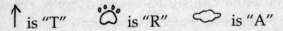

mysterious decoder
(The outer ring spins)

He reached for the library book, never taking his eyes off the decoder for a second. As he turned the wheel to find each symbol, I wrote down the letter translation in my journal:

↑ is "T"   ⚬ is "R"   ⌒ is "A"

In about two minutes, we had the whole message. Ian and I read it quickly. Then we looked at each other, frowning. We had it decoded, all right. But there was one slight problem.

What did it *mean*?

Chapter 13

Talk About a Walkabout!

I gazed down again at the message I'd written on my journal page:

"Traditional arts are not always true to traditional hearts."

Huh?
So far, my "Clues and Messages" list read:

"Traditional arts are not always true to traditional hearts."
"There is life in the coffins of the dead."
"Don't look in a usual boneyard."
Bone-pointing
My sketch of the painting

I marked the ones I thought might be definite clues with a star. The others I wasn't too sure about.

"What have we got so far, Hannah?" Ian asked.

I turned over my paper to hide my list and said nothing.

He caught on right away. "Hey, I'm sorry I was such a jerk about those messages before. Wherever they're coming from, now I know they're real. This code thing proves it."

"Apology accepted," I told him.

"Okay," he said. "Here are *my* clues so far." He handed me his spiral notebook. I handed him my journal page. It was probably a good idea to combine our ideas to see if together we could come up with something that made sense. Ian's notebook was all folded up and ratty. His list said:

1. Worth (American dollars): Oenpelli python—$30,000; shingleback skink—$2,500; black palm cockatoo—$20,000; rainbow lorikeet—$300
2. Large operation in the north
3. Poachers known to pay certain aboriginal artists for illegal work
4. Warehouse used for shipping

For a few minutes, we sat thinking. On their own, none of the things seemed to help us much. But if we put all of the pieces together...

"Hannah, I saw a poster for a bus tour leaving from the library today," Ian said suddenly. "It visits some of the traditional artists who work in northern Australia."

I nodded. "Sounds pretty interesting. Especially considering our coded message and your clue number three. When does the bus leave?"

Ian checked his watch. "In a half-hour," he said.

"Well, a bus tour can't be all that dangerous," I said with a grin. "I can handle that."

Ian smiled back at me. "Yeah, it's a tour for senior citizens. Sounds tame enough, doesn't it, mate?"

It sure did.

We paid for our tickets and boarded the bus with the senior citizens. They were so happy about having us coming along. "It'll be lovely to have you two youngsters on the trip," a man told us.

TRADITIONAL
ARTS BUS TOUR
-Bark Painters-
-Log Coffin Carvers-
-Musicians-

"You must be as fit as fiddles," said another. "Hope we can keep up with you."

"You are so brave, my dear," one lady said to me. "Are you and your brother traveling around Australia all on your own?"

They just couldn't say enough wonderful things about us.

Me   Winnie

I sat across the aisle from a nice woman who said her name was Winnie. It's short for Winifred. (Who would ever call their kid *that?*) She looked a lot like

Grandma Zoe, with her white hair all pulled back in a French twist. She was wearing red strawberry earrings and a beautiful pink shawl. She also had on hiking boots and thick cozy socks. Not exactly Grandma Zoe's style.

Winnie kept calling me "honey." I think she thought that was my name.

"My name is Hannah," I said for the second time.

"I know, honey," she said. "You told me that already."

"Right," I said.

"Are you on walkabout?" she asked.

"What's that?" I said.

"Oh, a walkabout is a very special journey," she said. "You go traveling about, here and there, discovering who you are while you see the world."

"You mean, like a vacation?" I asked.

"Heavens, no," Winnie said, laughing. "You might be gone months, even a year. And you don't send postcards."

"Don't people worry about you if you don't send postcards?" I asked, frowning. I thought of my parents back home. If I was gone for months or a year, they'd be pretty worried. With luck, my mission in Australia wasn't going to last that long and the angels would send me home. Not that I didn't like being here and all, but...

"If they worry, that's their problem," Winnie

said. I thought that was an unusual remark, especially coming from a senior citizen. Whoops! I'm not supposed to say "senior citizen." Grandma Zoe says it sounds cold, like a prison number or something. I'm supposed to say "older people."

"You know, *I'm* on walkabout," Winnie told me.

"You are?" I asked, surprised. "How old are you?" Whoops again! I clapped a hand over my mouth. "I'm sorry, that was really rude."

"Oh, fiddlesticks! I don't mind at all, honey," Winnie said. "Here in Australia, they call us older people 'wrinklies.' I just turned seventy-five. It's a wonderful age. I figure it's the perfect time for me to discover what I'll be contributing to the world in my next twenty-five years!"

Winnie sounded like Ms. Montgomery: *Every day is a brand-new day.*

"So, uh, aren't you supposed to *walk* on walkabout?" I asked.

"Oh, yes," she said. "Well, young people do. When an aboriginal boy turns sixteen, he goes on walkabout to find out what his reason is for being on this earth. He walks all the way, across deserts and mountains and rivers."

I wondered why only boys did walkabouts, not sheilas. On the other hand, Winnie was a grown-up sheila, and she was doing one.

"I take buses in between my walking, and trains and boats, too," she went on. "I figure now that I'm this old, I can cheat a little." She giggled.

I liked Winnie. When the bus reached the artist area, I figured maybe I could hang around with her. It was probably best for me and Ian to do our spy stuff separately, anyway.

As we got off the bus, I spotted a tree full of rainbow lorikeets. They were singing and chirping away. They were so pretty, all bright green and red and yellow and blue.

"Aren't they lovely?" Winnie said, standing beside me and looking up.

"Can you imagine," I said, "that poachers take these beautiful little birds away from their home, ship them across the ocean, and sell them for money?"

"How vile," Winnie said. She sounded angry and disgusted.

I liked that word. I pulled out my journal and wrote it down. It had the same letters as "evil," only mixed around. These poachers *were* vile. And they were evil.

VILE = EVIL

And I, Hannah Martin, was determined that Ian and I would succeed in stopping their vile, evil ways.

Chapter 14

Coffin of the Rainbow Serpent

"I'll tell you what I'm here for," Winnie whispered to me, with a twinkle in her eye.

"What?" I asked.

"To see the hollow-log coffins, honey," she said. "Have you ever seen one?"

I hadn't, but I immediately wanted to. Hollow-log coffins sounded very mysterious. I said good-bye to Ian and we agreed to find each other if we saw anything suspicious.

I followed Winnie to a small building where a group of artists were busy carving coffins. They didn't look like any coffins I'd ever seen before. They were made from very large logs, and they had designs all over them like the didgeridoos.

hollow-log coffins

"Just imagine, bodies go inside of those," Winnie said.

I didn't even want to think about that.

"Isn't that wonderful?" Winnie said.

I don't know if I'd call it "wonderful." I think "spooky" is a better word.

"Maybe I'll be buried in one," Winnie added, laughing.

"How can you talk like that?" I asked, horrified.

"Oh, honey, that won't be for ages and ages! You'll have five kids by then, and you'll be living in India, charming your cobras!" (I had told her on the bus about the cobras, and she said she could picture me as a snake charmer someday.)

"Look, there's a coffin with a rattlesnake on it," I said, pointing.

"That's not a rattlesnake, honey," said Winnie. "That's the rainbow serpent."

She explained that the designs the artists carved on the coffins told aboriginal dreamtime stories of the earth's creation.

"I know about the dreamtime!" I said, all excited. "It's how people fly with their feet on the ground."

Winnie nodded. "Well, yes. But that's just a part of the dreamtime. A tiny, tiny part. Dreamtime is also about the creation of the world and the animals you see in all this artwork. And the sacredness of our earth and…"

I could tell that Winnie could go on and on. And on.

"So the dreamtime's about everything?" I said. If I offered an ending to her story, she might wrap it up.

"That's right, honey," she said. "Dreamtime is about everything."

I got back to the point. "And the rainbow serpent?"

"The rainbow serpent," Winnie said, "is the symbol of healing. It created the rivers by crawling around at the beginning of time. The rainbow serpent helps medicine men heal people, and heal the whole earth. As you can see, many of these log coffins have the rainbow serpent on them."

That made me remember something. I pulled out my sketch from the market and looked back at the coffin. I had sketched the painting *wrong!* Remember how I thought the didgeridoo had been awfully wide and large? That's because it wasn't a didgeridoo. It was a hollow-log coffin! And the design wasn't a rattlesnake. It was a rainbow serpent! I scribbled a brand-new drawing on my journal page. I knew this had to be important. As soon as I found Ian, I'd tell him.

new drawing

We moved on from the coffins and passed some musicians in another part of the building. They were playing bilma sticks and boomerangs and bull-roarers. I was dying to show Winnie how I was learning the didgeridoo, so they let me borrow one for a minute. I got a sound out of it, a low buzzing hum. Winnie was as thrilled as I was.

twirling a
bull-roarer

In the middle of showing off my amazing new skill, a wind came up. Not from outside, but rustling through the didgeridoo. It was the same wind sound I'd heard that first night under the stars with George and Ian—and the same one I'd heard when I played my flute upside down. I was getting kind of used to things like this happening. I quickly put my ear on the opening.

"*Rush-sh-sh,*" a voice said. "*You are close-se-se.*"

I looked at Winnie. She hadn't heard anything. That's when I realized something that hadn't hit me before. This hush-voice wasn't Aurora's. It wasn't Demi's voice, either.

"Who are you?" I whispered back down the tube.

"*Leeeeeer-a,*" it answered.

"Are you an angel?" I whispered.

"*Yes-sss-sss,*" I heard back.

Now I had *three* angels! And this one, I knew, had to be a music angel. She was the one who'd transported me back and forth from music class, the one whose rustling sounds I heard whenever I played the flute or the didgeridoo. Leeera. In my head, I spelled it "Lyra." Like lyrical music.

RUSH...SH...SH

Lyra, my musical angel

Close! Lyra had said. So Ian and I were close. To the poachers? To the animals? And we had to *rush!* I had to find Ian immediately if not sooner.

"I have to go, Winnie!" I said, taking off at a run. "Catch you later!"

"What's wrong?" she called after me.

I had no time to answer. I tore out of the building and flew down the steps.

"Ian!" I shouted. He was right there on the landing, eating a chocolate cupcake. I nearly crashed into him. "Ian, we have to hurry," I said breathlessly. "We're onto something! We might be right near the p—"

He stuffed the cupcake into my mouth, shutting me up.

"I was afraid you were going to blow our cover," he whispered, glancing at all the people around us.

I swallowed the cupcake in one huge gulp. Good thing it was small! "Let's call them 'eggs' from now on," I whispered. "Code word for the bad guys."

"*Eggs?*" Ian looked at me as if I'd left my brains on the bus. "I don't know where you come up with this weird stuff, Hannah. But okay. So you think we're close to the...*eggs?*"

I nodded excitedly. "Yes."

"Well, where are they?" he asked.

"Tell me what you make of this," I said. I ripped out my sketch. "It wasn't a rattlesnake that I drew back in the marketplace, Ian! It was the rainbow serpent!"

He gave me a totally blank look. I stuck the paper right into his face.

"And it wasn't a didgeridoo, see? It was a hollow-log coffin!"

"I still don't get it," he said.

Ian could be really clueless sometimes. "Remember how I said the painting had an object that was wider than a real didgeridoo? And that it was important, but I wasn't sure why, but I sketched it and showed it to you?" The words were falling out of my mouth, tumbling all over each other. I wasn't making any sense.

"Slow down," he said, holding up his hand.

"The traditional art isn't a painting. It's a craft. It's the hollow-log coffins," I told him. "That's why there's life in the coffins of the dead. We're very close, Ian, very close."

"Hannah…"

Suddenly, I almost had a heart attack. Guess who was standing just a few yards away from us?

The golden-eyed man!

Chapter 15

Flat on My Face

He was standing right next to the building. He was so close, a good spit would have hit him. I grabbed Ian's arm and dug in my fingernails, hard.

"The golden-eyed man!" I whispered very softly. I tried to duck behind Ian so the man wouldn't see me. Luckily, he wasn't looking our way.

"I can't hear you, Hannah," Ian said.

I wanted to smack him! I leaned forward and whispered right in his face.

"The...golden...eyed...man!"

Ian's eyes widened in surprise. But when we looked back, the man had disappeared! We walked slowly to the end of the building and turned the corner. Sure enough, I wasn't imagining things. The golden-eyed man was getting into a Land Rover. He was wearing his blue denim vest and black boots and a cowboy hat.

Now I wasn't scared anymore. I thought of all those poor endangered animals and I took off like a shot. I had to catch this guy before his car pulled away and he disappeared on me again!

Ian must have started running the second after I did, because all of sudden…*Bam!* I was flat on my face in the dust. Ian had tackled me!

The tour people started to gather around us, chattering like cockatoos.

"Did you see that? My, my!"

"Well, isn't that boy full of spit and vinegar!"

"On the bus, they seemed so sweet!"

"Are you all right, honey?" It was Winnie. She reached out her hand to pull me to my feet. By this time, Ian was already up, brushing the dust from his jeans.

"You're a hopeless case, Hannah," he said, shaking his head. That's what my father always tells me. I'm incurable, like one of his sick dogs or something. (My dad's a veterinarian.)

HOPELESS CASE

DO NOT TREAT

"You didn't have to haul off and tackle me," I snapped angrily.

"Oh, yes, I did," Ian shot back. "You had to be stopped. There was no other way."

Now that I had a minute to think about it, I

realized he was right. What would I have done if I had caught the golden-eyed man before he drove off? He might have grabbed me and dragged me into his Jeep. Worse yet, he might have pointed a bone at me.

"I saw you go tearing off like a house afire, honey," said Winnie. "What was the emergency?"

I glanced at Ian. "I was just being a jerk," I told Winnie. "No fire. No reason."

"Well, let's go and find someplace to take care of those scrapes," Winnie said, examining my face and hands. Wasn't she the sweetest lady? She hardly even knew me, and here she was going to take care of my scrapes. But I couldn't go. I had to rush.

"Thanks, Winnie," I said, "but I'll be fine. I'm in a hurry to get somewhere."

Winnie's eyes lit up. She could tell there was an adventure brewing. We were a lot alike, Winnie and I.

Ian gave me a confused look. He still didn't have a clue as to what I was trying to tell him. I dragged him over to the hollow-log coffins.

The minute he saw them, it was as if he had been struck by a bolt of lightning. Everything dawned on him at once.

"Of course!" he said, thumping me on the back. "That's it!" He headed me away from the crowd toward a clump of trees.

"Why didn't I think of it before?" he said, still

all excited. "Those coffins hold the bones of the dead!"

"So if poachers are putting *animals* inside the coffins…" I began.

"…and shipping the coffins out of the country…!" Ian added.

"Then there *is* life…" I said.

"…in the coffins of the dead!" Ian finished.

Electricity was jumping between us. I felt as if I was all lit up, and you'd get a shock if you touched me.

It all made sense. The animals were probably being drugged or something to keep them quiet. Then they were put inside the hollow-log coffins and shipped out of the country! All the messages and clues fit.

"So where do they store the log coffins?" I asked.

Ian flipped open his spiral notebook. "In a warehouse, I guess," he said slowly. "There are a few of them just outside of town, on the water," he said.

"I *knew* we were close!" I exclaimed. (Of course I did—an angel had told me so.) "We have to hurry."

The seniors' tour bus wasn't leaving until six o'clock, and it was only two o'clock now. We couldn't possibly wait for four hours! No way. We'd left the Jeep parked at the library back in Alligator Bay. What were we going to do?

"Let's check with the bus driver," Ian said. "We don't have time to go back and get the Jeep."

The driver was reading a magazine. He had nothing to do until it was time for the bus to go back. We paid him ten dollars to drive us to the waterfront. For another ten dollars, he agreed to come back and pick us up at five-thirty. This mission was getting expensive. But now we had a good three hours to investigate.

Ian and I got off the bus and looked around. A string of buildings, all rusty and run-down, lined

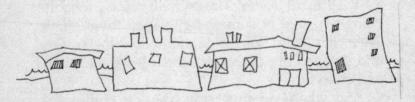

the waterfront. It was starting to drizzle, and I felt a little jumpy. Even though we didn't see anyone around, there was danger in the air. I could also feel danger in the water. *And* in the wobbly old buildings. I could practically smell Mr. Golden Eye, lying in wait for us.

"If this is where the—the *eggs*—are operating, I'm scared, Ian," I said.

"Me too," he said. "Remember, we just want to find evidence. We don't want to actually meet up with any...eggs."

"I think we need a plan," I said.

"Yeah, we do," Ian said, thinking. "Wasn't there a whistle in that pack of yours, Hannah?"

"I think I saw one when we dumped everything out in the library," I said. I took off my knapsack, dug through it for a minute, and pulled out a large, shiny whistle.

"A police whistle," Ian said. "Not bad, mate. That sound will carry a long way to alert someone if we need help."

Angels think of absolutely everything, I guess. I passed the whistle to Ian and he hung it around his neck.

"We'll stay together every minute," he said. "No separating. Got that?"

I got it. Here we were, right in the heart of poacher territory. We couldn't afford any mistakes.

"I'll be in charge of protecting us. You be in charge of marking down evidence in your journal, okay?"

"Okay," I said. This time, I didn't get mad at Ian for being bossy.

"We can investigate each warehouse, one at a time," Ian said. "Ready?"

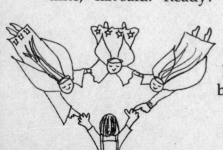

Ready, angels? I said silently. I wanted Aurora to guide me, Lyra to transport me back if I got in terrible trouble, and Demi to be right here at my side every step of the way.

"*Yes,*" I heard a voice say. I felt it more than heard it, like it was all three angels together. I looped my thumbs through the straps of my backpack and took a deep breath.

"Ready," I said.

Chapter 16

The Key to My Mission

We moved from one building to the next, with Ian leading and me following. It would be too risky for us to be out in open view. The first warehouse was empty, except for the mice skittering around on the floor. Usually, I don't mind mice, but I get all twitchy when they're running around my feet.

I made a note:

Warehouse #1—Empty, with mice

"Next building," Ian whispered. I nodded.

We crept out the side door of the mouse warehouse and dashed quickly to the door of the next building. It was locked.

Plastering ourselves against the rusting metal walls, we inched our way around the outside of the building. The next door was locked, too. And the next. We went around the back, by the water, and found a large window that had been painted over so you couldn't see inside. Ian pushed on it—and it opened!

I took a deep breath, my heart pounding. I was terrified! Ian went in first, then he reached back to help me climb through. I jumped to the floor. Inside, it was pitch-dark. I could hear a few birds or bats swooping through the room.

We stood perfectly still so our eyes could adjust to the darkness.

"Flashlight," Ian whispered.

Luckily, I had hooked it onto the outside of my pack. I unhooked it and turned it on. Slowly, I flashed the light around the room. There, right in front of us, was a hollow-log coffin with a picture of the rainbow serpent on it.

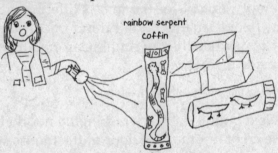

rainbow serpent
coffin

"Bingo!" Ian cried. "This is it!"

Just then, I froze. I'd heard a noise. It was a quiet rustling that was coming from somewhere right by the rainbow serpent. I saw Ian go for the police whistle. He clamped it between his teeth, just in case.

I flashed the light in the direction of the rustling, feeling really nervous. There were log coffins—tons and tons of them—piled up all over the place. But I didn't see anything moving.

After a moment or two, the rustling stopped. Good. I shone the light on the floor in front of me. There was an empty space between me and the rainbow serpent coffin. I took a step toward the coffin. I just had to see what was inside.

Suddenly, something hit my legs. I tripped and crashed to the floor. The flashlight went skidding backward.

Then I heard Demi's voice. "Stop!" she commanded. "Danger."

I crawled back up against the window as Ian snatched up the flashlight.

He shone it on the floor, right in front of the rainbow serpent. There was a snake, slithering across the concrete, heading straight for me! It wasn't a python, and it wasn't a cobra.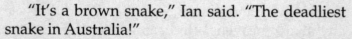

"It's a brown snake," Ian said. "The deadliest snake in Australia!"

Both of us leapt up on a wooden box and watched the snake slink its way along the floor. It flickered in the beam of the flashlight, then slithered out through a hole at the base of the window.

Shaking with fear, I let out a huge breath—and a loud sob.

"We've got our evidence, Hannah," Ian said. "Let's get out of here."

"B-b-but, Ian," I said, still shaking so much that my teeth chattered. "It's not exactly evidence."

"It's close enough, Hannah," Ian said.

"We don't know for sure if there are animals in these coffins," I pointed out.

"True, but George can check that out," Ian said.

I wanted to get out of there. But I wanted to stay, too. I really needed to see if the coffins had endangered animals inside.

"What should we do, Ian?" I whispered. "This is really scary, but we're so close. How can we leave now?"

Ian was silent. I could tell he felt the same way I did.

"Let's just look inside one of them, Ian," I pleaded. "Then we can go."

Ian flashed the beam of light on the coffins, checking for more brown snakes. We didn't see any, thank heavens. He beamed the light up and down on the rainbow serpent coffin. There was something strange on the top. A padlock!

"Do they always put locks on log coffins?" I whispered.

"No way," said Ian, shaking his head.

"But poach—uh, eggs might put locks on coffins, right?" I said.

"That's the only possible answer," Ian said.

For a moment, we didn't budge. We just stared at each other in the darkness, thinking the same thing. We knew we had to check out the coffins. How could we come all this way and turn back before we knew for sure? We listened for any more unusual noises, but we heard only the birds and the bats flapping around.

Very carefully, we stepped down off the wooden box and crept our way toward the coffin. Ian reached out and pulled it toward him, taking a hold of the lock.

"Give me the key," he said.

"Key?" I asked. *Key!* Of course! The rusty old key I'd found in my pocket at the restaurant this morning!

I reached into my pocket and pulled it out. Without a word, I handed it to Ian. And then, very carefully, he jiggled the key in the lock.

Chapter 17

Lorikeet Kisses

This is probably a weird time to bring up my dog Frank, but I kept thinking about him the whole time Ian was trying the key. When Frank was a puppy, I took one look at him, and I knew he had to be mine. He was the runt of the litter, and he had one blind eye. But I didn't care. He was the cutest puppy on earth and I just *had* to have him. I couldn't eat or sleep or anything else until April Fools' Day (that's my birthday). That was the day my parents gave me Frank.

That's how much I wanted this key to work, the way I'd wanted my dog. I held the flashlight and Ian kept wriggling the key. It seemed like it was never going to fit that rusty padlock. Finally, Ian turned the key. The lock opened!

We both held our breath. He twisted the padlock off the top of the coffin. He opened the coffin, and I beamed the light inside.

The coffin was stuffed with rags. Carefully, I unwrapped the folds on the top rag. I gasped. There was a rainbow lorikeet inside! It looked as if it was asleep.

"It's been drugged," Ian said.

Just then, we heard a car engine outside. I grabbed Ian's arm. The two of us stood frozen, listening.

The car rolled over the gravel, pulling up outside the warehouse. We heard a door slam and the sound of footsteps. Someone was heading right toward the window in front of us!

A shadow crossed the window. Ian set the coffin carefully on the floor, and I flipped the flashlight off. We hid ourselves behind a pile of coffins in the corner.

The window creaked open as someone stepped inside the warehouse. Someone big.

We shouldn't have done this, I thought. *We should have quit while we were safe. Now we're trapped, just like that poor little bird inside its coffin cage!*

A flashlight beamed from the window, then

over the coffins above our heads and around the room.

Suddenly, I heard a new sound. The lorikeet had woken up, and it was saying, "G'day, mate! G'day, mate!" clear as day.

The footsteps approached the rainbow serpent coffin, which was only a few feet from our hiding place. Then they stopped. I could hear shuffling as someone reached down to pick up the coffin with the squawking bird in it.

I had to see what was happening. I peeked out through a crack between the coffins. I could just make out the shadow of a man. He set the flashlight on a box and lifted the coffin. The beam of light caught his face. His eyes flashed gold!

I grabbed Ian and we crouched there, not budging an inch. We held on to each other like it was our last moment on earth.

Where are you, angels? I called silently. *Aurora? Lyra? Demi?*

I could still see out through the crack. Now the golden-eyed man was reaching inside the coffin and taking out the lorikeet. But he did it gently, and he lifted the bird right up to his face. Then he actually gave that lorikeet two sweet little kisses on the beak.

"G'day, mate," he said to the bird.

The bird just lay in his hands, squawking weakly. "G'day, mate," it said back.

In the beam of the light, I could see the man's face very clearly. A tear trickled down his cheek.

"You poor little creature," he said, stroking the bird's feathers. "You poor, sad little bird."

I couldn't believe it! The evil golden-eyed man had *tears* in his eyes. What was going on?

Just then, a voice boomed through the window. It was no angel's either.

"Who goes there?" it bellowed, echoing off the walls.

In a flash, Golden Eye scrambled into the pile of coffins right beside us!

Chapter 18

Poaching May Be Hazardous to Your Health

We heard a key rattling in the back door. The door was flung open, and rainy light rushed into the warehouse. I squinted in the brightness.

"Come out with your hands behind your heads!" the voice boomed.

"This is the law!"

I grabbed Ian tighter.

"This is the law!" the voice shouted.

The golden-eyed man stood up, squinting just like me. He had the little lorikeet tucked safely in his hands.

The other person, whoever he was, walked boldly in Golden Eye's direction. Suddenly, he stopped.

"Hey, Goldie!" he shouted. "Is that you?"

The golden-eyed man grinned from ear to ear. "Skinkman!" he yelled gleefully. "Am I ever glad to see you, mate!"

Skinkman?

I heard Ian let out his breath.

Golden Eye practically leapt over the coffins, still clutching the lorikeet. He wrapped his free arm around George. George gave him a big bear hug back. They were laughing and hugging like old buddies. "You can come out now, mates!" Golden Eye called.

He'd known we were there the whole time, I guess. Ian and I stood up.

I thought George was going to wring our necks. He looked really, really mad.

"What are you two doing here?" he asked.

Ian and I exchanged guilty looks. Then we both started talking at once. We told George how we were sorry, but we were happy we found the animals, and we were scared because we thought Goldie was a poacher, and on and on. The two of us just couldn't shut up.

George held up his hands in surrender.

"Okay, okay," he said. "I'm glad you both lived to tell me about all this. Let me introduce Buzz Thompson."

Goldie extended his birdless hand for a shake. We shook hands.

"Mr. Thompson is an ecologist," said George. "He and I have been on the trail of these poachers for years."

"I heard you kids talking at Tiny's yesterday, behind George's back," said Goldie. "I thought you were in cahoots with poachers!"

I laughed with relief. "And I thought *you* were a poacher," I said, "following us around like that!"

"Well, it worked out fine, didn't it? You mates led me right to this warehouse!" Goldie said. He really did sound grateful.

"How did you know about this place, George?" asked Ian.

"Goldie tipped me off," said George. "I followed him here. In fact, I had a feeling I'd meet up with you two."

"So Goldie followed us, and you followed Goldie!" Ian said.

"And I was scared you were going to point a bone at me and kill me," I admitted to Goldie. I saw now that his eyes were a warm brown, tinged with gold. The gold flecks glimmered in the sunlight. Actually, they were kind of pretty up close.

Goldie frowned. "Bone-pointing is no joke," he said. "It's very serious. After these poachers get arrested, a medicine man may indeed decide to punish them with a bone-pointing."

"They've broken sacred laws," George

pointed out. "They'll have to pay for the terrible damage they've caused."

"Oh," I said. I almost felt sorry for them. For just a minute.

"Yes," Goldie agreed. "These blokes are bad eggs."

"Bad *eggs*, all right," Ian said, nudging me.

I glared at him, but I wasn't really mad. I guess that egg idea of mine *was* a little dorky.

"Let's get to work," George said. Using my key, we opened one coffin after the next. We found dozens of lorikeets, cockatoos, and skinks. In the two largest coffins, we discovered two Oenpelli pythons! You'd have to see one to believe how huge it is. It stretched from one warehouse door to the next!

Right away, George got on his cell phone. First he called about the animals.

"Send over a team pronto," he said. "We've hit the jackpot! We've got to make sure these critters are all right and get them straight home where they belong."

Next, George called the police. "I got a tip that the poachers will be shipping out of a waterfront warehouse tonight." He gave them the address. "Bring plenty of backup. We'll arrest every last one of them."

When he finally got off the cell phone, we gave one another high-fives. Everybody started

high-fives
(just kidding!)

thumping everybody else on the back.

"Good job, mates," said George.

"Good job, mates," the lorikeet said.

Then George came over and gave me and Ian one big bear hug. What a great guy he was, saving all these animals!

"Now you mates get lost," he told us. "I don't want you around when we take these blokes down tonight. You got that?"

Just then, the seniors' tour bus pulled up for Ian and me. And at the very same moment, I heard Lyra's music. It swirled around me until I felt myself begin to float off.

And guess what?

Good job, mates

Chapter 19

How Many Angels Does One Kid Need?

Suddenly, I was back in music class. But this time, there was no chaos. No skunk hair. No scraping.

I was sitting in the same spot that I had before I'd left. To my surprise, the rest of the class was huddled in a far corner of the room. They were staring at me, absolutely terrified.

"It's gone!" Jimmy Fudge shouted.

"What's gone?" I asked.

"The snake, of course," said Ms. Crybaby.

"*What* snake?" I said. "What's the matter with all of you?"

"Hannah! There was a gigantic snake wrapped around you a second ago," Katie said, running toward me. "I was so scared for you!"

"It was huge!" someone else said. Then everybody started talking at once.

"It looked like a boa!"

"No, it had to be a python!"

"It was *incredible!*"

"The longest snake I've ever seen!"

"It had to be twenty feet long. You were totally wound up in it, Hannah!"

I began to get an idea of what was going on. Had the angels sent an Oenpelli python back with me from Australia?

"It must have escaped from Mr. Schneider's science class," I said lamely.

"No way!" Jimmy Fudge insisted. "That was no wimpy little science class snake!"

"I wonder where it went," said Kevin, frowning. He and Jimmy started searching under the desks and between the music stands. Now they were being all brave, I guess.

"Hannah, what's that you're holding?" Katie asked then.

I looked down. I had my flute in one hand— and a didgeridoo in the other!

I smiled.

"It's an Australian instrument," I said. "A didgeridoo."

"A *what?*" the whole class said at once.

Everyone gathered around me, even Jimmy Fudge. They were buzzing with excitement like a swarm of black flies.

"I've never seen a didgeridoo," said Ms. Crybaby. "May I try it?" she asked.

"Sure. I'll show you how," I said.

My teacher sat on the floor cross-legged. Ms. Crybaby, sitting on the floor! Can you believe it? It was totally unlike her to actually have fun with us sixth graders.

I showed her how to hum and *pfffttt*. She was *pffftt*ting and laughing and laughing and *pffftt*ting, all at once. It was amazing. Then everybody wanted to try the didgeridoo.

"Cool hat, Hannah," somebody said.

Hat? I felt my head. I'd come back with the Aussie souvenir that Ian had bought for me at the market!

"Where'd you get all this stuff, Hannah?"

"And what are those animals on the didgeridoo?"

I answered the second question, but not the first.

"They're all endangered animals in Australia," I told them.

"Hey, that snake looks like the one that was wrapped around you a minute ago."

"It was so odd," Ms. Crybaby chimed in. "That enormous snake just disappeared into thin air."

I told everyone about the Oenpelli python and how it could change colors, and how poachers kidnap them and sell them for big bucks. I told them about the other animals on the didgeridoo: the skinks and rainbow lorikeets.

But there was one thing I didn't tell them. I didn't say a word about my angels. I mean, who would believe me, anyway?

After school, Katie and David cornered me on the way home. They boxed me in, one on my right side, one on my left. Then they started pushing in on me, squeezing.

"She'll talk under torture," David said.

"Come on, Hannah," said Katie. "Tell us what happened."

"What are you guys talking about?" I said innocently.

"Hannah, I know that's not your hat!" Katie said. Of course she knew that. Katie knows every last piece of clothing I own. She's worn most of them at least once.

"So where did you get this hat, Hannah?" David asked, taking it from me and plopping it on his head.

It looked pretty good on him. Great, in fact. Everything looks good on David.

"Oh, it just showed up, I guess," I said.

"In the middle of music class?" Katie gave me a sideways look. "You're lying," she said. "Like a rug."

"No, really," I insisted. "It's a long story."

"I have time," Katie said.

But I wasn't ready to tell her everything yet,

even though she was my best friend. I needed to let all of this mission stuff soak in a little.

"Hey, what's this?" David asked. He'd taken off the hat and pulled out a piece of bark from inside. It had tiny painted marks all over it.

"It looks like some kind of code!" he said, intrigued. "I've never seen anything like this!"

Katie and I looked at it. It said:

There was a signature after it, all flowing and beautiful. It said, "Love, Lorielle."

"Who's Lorielle?" Katie asked, snatching the bark from David.

"Maybe it's the name of the hat maker," I said. But I knew better.

I'd been wondering who'd sent me the coded message at the library. It didn't seem like anything Aurora or Demi or Lyra would do. It was a totally different style of message.

I smiled to myself. I had a *fourth* angel! I must really be a problem kid, to need help from *four* angels!

"Hannah, we have to talk," Katie said, catching me by the arm.

"We will," I said. "I promise."

"When?" she asked.

"Tomorrow," I said.

Right now I wanted to be alone. I had to get home and see my parents and Frank. I had to decode Lorielle's message. I had to take a little time to thank my angels, all *four* of them. And I figured I'd better rest up.

After all, who knows when my angels might come around again? And when angels call, you've got to drop everything and just go.

You know what I mean?

Cheers, mate!

Aborigine - The word we use for all the native Australian people, whose families have lived there for over 40,000 years. There are many, many groups of Australian aborigines, including the Koori, Yamadji, Larrakeyah, and Bunuba. All these words mean "people" in the language of each group.

Australian dollar - The currency (money) used in Australia.

Bark painting - Paintings made on pieces of tree bark, mostly by the aborigines in northern Australia. Many of the pictures of animals and people look like x-rays, since you can see the bones, heart, lungs, and other internal body parts in the painting.

Bone-pointing - (Scary!) A ceremony, performed by a medicine man, to kill someone who has broken sacred laws. It's kind of like capital punishment and stirs up the same differences of opinion. A bone from the leg of a kangaroo is pointed at the offender, taking the soul from his body. The target becomes sicker and sicker, and eventually dies.

Boomerang - A flat, curved weapon usually made of wood, used for hunting and fighting. Boomerangs are also used as musical instruments. They make a clacking sound when two of them are hit together. Mostly, we use boomerangs for fun, because when we throw them, they fly through the air and return to us.

Bull-roarer - A piece of wood attached to a cord that's used as a musical instrument. You twirl it around your head to make a whirring noise, like roaring wind or thunder.

Cockatoo - A parrotlike bird with a crest of feathers on its head. Some cockatoos are common in Australia and are a nuisance to farmers because they eat their crops. Others, like the black palm cockatoo, are endangered.

Colors - Red, black, yellow, and white are sacred colors to the aborigines. Red means fire, black means earth, yellow means water, and white means stars.

Darwin - A city in northern Australia on the Timor Sea. It is tropical (north is hot and south is cold below the equator) and looks like a Wild West town, with people dressed in cowboy clothes.

Didgeridoo - A musical instrument, about four or

five feet long, made of wood that's been hollowed out by termites. Each particular aboriginal group paints didgeridoos differently. Some use earth colors, like brown, rust, and ocher. Others prefer bright purples, reds, and greens. In some groups, women are forbidden to play the didgeridoo. Many people believe that certain sacred didgeridoos play themselves (giving the musicians the music, instead of the other way around). You play the didgeridoo by blowing into it.

Dingo - A wild dog that looks something like a German shepherd and hunts at night, sometimes in groups. They howl a LOT.

Dreaming - The aborigines believe ancient beings come to us in our dreams. They bring messages to help us live our lives in a good way. These same ancient beings spoke to our grandparents, our great-grandparents, and all our ancestors. Every aboriginal child is born with a special Dreaming, like Skink Dreaming or Yam Dreaming or Crocodile Dreaming.

Dreamtime - The beginning of the world, when the aborigines believe ancient beings gave everything important to the world: the lakes and the mountains, the animals, the art, the songs and dances. Aborigines know how to enter the Dreamtime without going to sleep. (It's a little like meditation.) By "dreaming," they learn ancient secrets people have forgotten.

Ghost gum tree - A type of eucalyptus tree that has white bark, a lot like birch trees back home. Australia has many species of gum trees.

Hollow-log coffin - A coffin used by the aboriginal people of northern Australia to bury the bones of their dead. The coffins stand upright, like tree trunks, and they're painted with pictures of animals and spirits.

Kangaroo - (Bet you know this one!) A large hopping animal, called a *marsupial* because it carries its babies in its pouch. A young kangaroo is called a "joey." (Cute, huh?)

Koala - (These are cute, too.) A gentle marsupial that sleeps most of the day and eats eucalyptus leaves most of the night. Their aboriginal name means "not drinking water." (By the way, koalas are not bears.)

Oenpelli - An area of northern Australia that has been returned to the aborigines and is inhabited by several groups. The endangered Oenpelli python lives here.

Outback - The huge, hot, reddish area in the middle and western part of Australia that makes up two-thirds of the entire country. The Outback is mostly flat desert, with weird, beautiful rock formations. In the wet season, sudden freak storms cause floods. Only fifteen percent of Australians live in the Outback.

Ownership philosophy - The aborigines believe that everything we own belongs to everyone else, the animals belong to everyone, and land cannot be bought or sold because it belongs to everyone.

Python - A non-poisonous snake that kills its prey by coiling around it and suffocating it. The Oenpelli python, which grows up to twenty-five feet long and changes colors to protect itself, is an endangered species in Australia.

Rainbow lorikeet - A small parrot with a reddish beak and red, yellow, green, and blue feathers. Even though they are an endangered species, they are sometimes smuggled overseas for money.

Rainbow serpent - A huge water snake from aboriginal mythology with fangs, scales, and a mane on its head. It crawled across the land at the beginning of time, carving out mountains and rivers in its path. You can see its picture on paintings and hollow-log coffins.

Skink - An endangered lizard that looks more like a snake, with a narrow body and very short legs.

Songlines - Musical "paths" from the aboriginal Dreamtime. Songlines are like storylines, telling the stories of the ancestors without using words. The aborigines believe their ancestors wandered the land in ancient times, singing the names of birds and plants, rocks and rivers, until everything came to life from their singing. Songs played by musicians tell about these Dreamtime adventures.

Stockman - An Australian cowboy.

Swag - A canvas mat with two big flaps, used as a sleeping bag when you travel in the Outback. A *swagman* is an Outback wanderer.

Termite hills - (Amazing!) Hard-packed hills built by large termites in northern Australia. Sometimes they're over six feet tall. They're always built in a north-south direction. That way, the ants can control their heating and cooling systems.

Tuckerbag - A bag that holds *tucker* (the Aussie slang for food) when you travel in the Outback.

Walkabout - A journey in which you follow paths across the Outback, using the stars and the earth to guide you. Aborigines walk until they finally enter the Dreamtime, where their ancestors live. Back home, we might think of a walkabout as a long journey to find our true selves and our reason for being born.

Wallaby - An animal similar to a kangaroo, but smaller.

Wombat - A stocky marsupial that looks like a small bear.

Yam - A vegetable, similar to a sweet potato, that is an important food for the aborigines. In many aborigine stories, yams turn into women or women turn into yams. (I'm not sure why!)

Here's a sneak peek at

Hannah and the Angels #2:
Searching for Lulu

Available now wherever books are sold!

Now what? I was stumped. Here I was, somewhere in Kenya, with no idea what to do or where to go—and poor Mcheshi was getting sicker and sicker!

I pulled out my journal and jotted down my clues:

Green
Lulu
Pearl

For some reason, I decided to sketch a picture of the queen piece from my chess game with David back home. As soon as I started drawing, I heard familiar music in the far distance. It was my angel Lyra playing, for sure.

I kept on drawing and the music got louder. This was amazing!

I drew faster and faster. I sketched the queen's hair, then her face. The minute I finished, I was completely surrounded by the music. I knew what that meant: Lyra was sending me some-place—and I had no idea where.

Suddenly, I was back home again, sitting across the chessboard from David. We were right where we'd left off in our game.

"Checkmate!" he said, all smug.

For once, I didn't even care that David had won. I was clutching the queen chess piece exactly the way I had been when the angels whisked me to Kenya. And I *knew*—I just knew— that Lyra was telling me something important.

Did I have the answer right in my hand?

Earn Your Golden Wings!

If you've acted like Hannah and helped someone else, you are eligible to receive a special *Hannah and the Angels* golden wings gift. Fill out the coupon below with details of how you acted like an angel (attach additional sheets if necessary).

To receive your FREE gift, mail to:

Random House Children's Publishing
Earn Your Wings Promotion
201 East 50th Street, MD 30-2
New York, NY 10022

- -

Name: _____ Age: _____

Address: _____

_____

I was an angel when I _____

_____

_____

_____

_____